I0576007

Thrall

By J.T. McGee

Valenza Publishing

Valenza Publishing
Hadley, NY 12835

First published in 2021
First Edition published 2024
Second Edition published 2025

ISBN:
Paperback - 979-8-9919345-5-8
E-book - 979-8-9891368-4-1

Praise for J.T. and Thrall

"...compelling for crime and supernatural fiction fans, offering a unique blend of mystery, character-driven drama, and a hint of the otherworldly. It's a book that transcends the typical boundaries of its genre, providing a suspenseful, engaging, and thoroughly captivating reading experience."
-Overly Honest Reviews, @overlyhonestmoviereviews

"This book was a fun, quick read, especially for those who love elements of horror, and mythical/supernatural lore. I had a fun time reading this book, and in the best way, it was a fast finish."
-Jade Nioma, author of "Fate's Tether"

"...a fantastic read, and a great debut from the author, perfect for spooky season. My only complaint is that I would love to read more."
-J.M. Gokey, author of "The Chosen"

More by Valenza Publishing

Dedication

Incredibly grateful to my family, friends, and students for their support.

CHARLES CROSS

Red and blue lights lit up the columned front of the summer home. The mansion's white pillars swirled in the light like psychedelic barber's poles. The house belonged to the Cross family. It sat in a regal splendor; a large Victorian nestled between other grand homes along North Broadway. The summer brought all sorts of activity to Saratoga, but never anything like this. Inside, Charles Cross' body lay on its side exsanguinate, his lower jaw nearly ripped off.

The normally quiet end of Broadway abruptly stops at the entrance to Skidmore College. Lavish homes dot either side of the road and owning a residence along it is reserved for the wealthy. Other than the normal activity associated within the proximity of a college, it was usually bathed in a stately tranquility. It was now ablaze with police lights and the squawk and buzz of radio communication.

Detective Madson pulled up to the house and parked diagonally. His car was a flat brown Caprice that was older than his college-bound son. The car was kept in impeccable condition and running smoothly thanks to the efforts of his partner, Becker, who was riding shotgun. The car tilted sideways as Madson's nearly three-hundred-pound frame struggled to stand. The shocks cringed and squeaked amidst grunts of protest as Madson pulled himself from the vehicle. In the meantime, Becker had made his way around to the front of the car before Madson had even closed his door. Becker smoothed his khakis with his palms as he waited for his partner to extract himself.

"What's the parade for?" Madson quipped as he pulled up his pants and adjusted his revolver.

"This is a big deal, this guy had money." Becker retorted, pushing his glasses into place on his nose as he moved past men and women in uniform taping off the sidewalk.

"The August place to be…" Madson grumbled as he moved in his bulldog-like shuffle to follow Becker.

"More like the whole summer now that they extended racing season," Becker replied as he turned the doorknob, holding the door open for Madson to head inside the house.

The flash of cameras mimicked the lights from the squad cars outside. Forensics swarmed the body, taking photos from every imaginable angle. There were tiny, numbered tents near drops of blood. They moved away from the body towards the hallway at the rear of the living room. Extinguished pillar candles sat in a wide circle around the body, white drops of dried wax pooled on the hardwood floor. Madson wasn't bothered by blood, he had seen blood before. Over time one even becomes accustomed to the smell of death. He was struck by how differently this scene smelled.

Yet instantly he was struck by something amiss. It wasn't

even the smell. Amidst the commotion one thing stood out; it was all too clean. The high vaulted ceilings were free of blemishes, pristinely white walls without a mar, every knickknack (although there were few) were upright, and nothing was out of place. Even the pillows were undisturbed and lying in a symmetrical arrangement on the ends of the mahogany leather sofa as if no one had sat down.

Madson shot a puzzled look at Becker with a crooked bushy black eyebrow and said, "Smells like low tide in here," under his breath. Normally a homicide scene had a peculiar smell like rust or old batteries. This room had none of the usual scents associated with a dead body.

"Reminds me of my vacations at the Cape as a kid," Becker added with a smirk that twisted his ginger-brown mustache.

Only this isn't Cape Cod, it's Saratoga in August. Hours from the ocean, Madson thought to himself.

Madson and Becker walked directly towards the body, past a throng of uniformed wall flowers. There were three people around the body leaning in with swabs, dabbing at it and poking around with tweezers. Their latex gloved hands moved slow and steady. Their movements became accentuated by the strobe light flash of cameras. Shots were being taken from multiple perspectives.

As the detectives came in, they were greeted by cops in uniform. The officers whispered to one another after the detectives passed. This was a huge case, and any involvement could mean a promotion. They didn't dare get in the way of Madson as he worked and eyed him cautiously. The detective's reputation for operating with a stern no-nonsense approach preceded him.

Madson towered over a crime scene guy as he pulled a thermometer out of the corpse's liver. He noticed that the jaw was hanging half off and there were two deep lacerations on either cheek. Madson struggled to kneel beside the body. Slowly he pulled his pen from his shirt pocket. Williams, the investigator, turned to face him, snapped from his focus on the body by the invasion of space. Madson pointed to the right cheek of Charles Cross. Two horizontal lacerations ran from below the ear to the corner of his mouth. The flesh was torn in a jagged zigzag and pieces of his cheek flapped open exposing his teeth beneath.

Madson called to the photographer, "Get a shot of this!"

A flash followed his directive. He struggled to his feet once more and moved to the other side of the body. Hunkering down again, he lifted the side of the head with his pen. There was another set of nearly identical marks.

"What the hell is this?" Madson realized a little too late that he had spoken aloud. The wall flowers scurried in and craned their necks to see what he was talking about. Getting to his feet, he tried to straighten himself both physically and mentally, hiking up his pants and shifting his piece. He had always been built like a gorilla, but as he grew older he had packed some pounds onto his midsection. He was quite the contrast to his partner who was slim, neat, somewhat mousy, and of average height.

"What's the good word, Williams?" Madson asked.

"This guy's been dead since last night around seven," Williams reported, "but there's something else."

"What is it? You got any idea what happened to him?"

"Actually, I'm clueless. But I can tell you this, he's about four pints low."

"Of blood ?" Becker asked.

"Yeah, he's bone dry, a few drops on the floor. He is pretty much empty of all fluids."

Madson rubbed his balding head, "Where the hell is all the blood?"

Madson moved away from the body. Not only did he feel foolish for drawing attention to himself, but also a little cramped with the rush of lookey-loos. He never cared for crowds or tight spaces, ever since he was little. He moved towards the fireplace and leaned on the mantle. Black marble with flecks of mica and veins of an amber color, it was cool beneath his hands. He noticed heat on his shins. He looked down and a few embers were blinking in and out in the charred hunks of wood. He hadn't smelled the fire; the front door was now standing open, and the smell of the scene must have overpowered it. From the look of the remnants, it had been a raging fire.

Madson feigned a cough to get Becker's attention. Once he made eye contact, he kicked his foot at the fireplace. Becker nodded quizzically, but affirmatively. Years of working together had its benefits, one of which was subtle communication. Madson patted the mantle, his school ring clinking metallically against the stone. The mantle was devoid of any decoration, except for one photo in a frame. It was in the center laid face down. Madson awkwardly tipped it up with his pen.

"Need some prints here."

The photo was of Charles Cross, a silver-haired man with a devilish grin and old-Hollywood good looks. He stood, arms outstretched around two young men, one dark-haired and preppy while the other sported stubble and a buzz cut. They were undoubtedly his sons. Madson recognized the family and the scenery. The rose gardens at Yaddo, an artists' retreat just beyond Saratoga's Thoroughbred racetrack. The place had a tragic and lonely history of its own, a history of untimely death.

"What kind of trouble did you get yourself into Charles?" Madson muttered under his breath to the picture. He rested his forehead on his fists whispering, "And now I've got to go talk to your boys."

Madson had a son of his own but the thought of questioning the boys after they had lost their father bothered him. He waved to Becker, saying, "Beck, let's get some air."

They moved to the door. The routine was the same for years. To the car, they went to go over the situation and to enjoy the air conditioning. Madson got in first, pulling the door closed with one hand and simultaneously loosening his tie with the other. Becker followed, waving to another squad car as it passed.

Madson was lost in thought. This was big. In his seventeen years of being a detective, he had never seen anything like this. A homicide might come along once every three or four summers. With all the tourists and workers coming up from New York City and who knows where else, all the growth the city has seen over the past ten years, it was a matter of probability and time that homicides would occur.

This wasn't anything like that. This wasn't just a homicide. This town wasn't ready for something like this; hell, Madson wasn't ready for something like this.

"What's up?" Becker quipped although he knew the drill. The question pulled Madson from his thoughts.

"Okay, so this guy's jaw is nearly ripped off, right?"

"Yup," Becker replied, "dangling."

"But his body wasn't twisted up or beat up. There were no bruises on his face and no defensive wounds on his hands. He was just kneeling there like he knew what was coming like it was inevitable. There were no signs of a struggle, the house wasn't trashed, and not a thing was missing."

"Nope, not so far."

Madson couldn't help but think that nothing would turn up missing.

"No broken windows or doors forced open."

"Nope."

"No ropes or cuffs, nothing to show that he was held against his will while somebody did this to him."

"No, he had a ring of candles around him."

"Candles, and a fire going, in August. No power outages last night. Who would stoke up a fire in this weather? It wasn't cold last night."

"Not at all. The missus had two fans and the A.C. running in the bedroom."

"Maybe something will turn up when they're done going over the house."

As if on cue, there was a tap at the window. A cop in uniform leaned in smiling nervously.

"What?" Madson grumbled.

"Uh, sorry, Sir. Um, Williams sent me to get you."

"Okay, what is it?"

"The team found something in the basement they wanted you to see."

"The basement?"

"Uh well, the wine cellar actually, some kind of hole in the wall or something."

Madson jumped from the car so quickly that his car door nearly toppled the rookie. The door bounced off the young officer's knees and Madson was up the steps before he could even yelp. Becker moved in his usual controlled pace regarding what had transpired. Becker was clearly impressed at how fast Madson could move when he wanted to. He smirked and shrugged at the limping officer as they headed to the door.

NATHAN CROSS

Vertical streams of rainwater slithered down the window that separated Nathan Cross from the rest of the city below him. The office was dark and empty. Cubicles and carpeting draped in shadows. The light from the marquis gave the tenth floor of the firm a sort of lonely phosphorescence. Bill Russell was the last person to leave. It was August 20th, the day before his son's birthday. Bill had stayed late to sign cards and condense his gifts into festive bags. He hadn't noticed Nathan's snoring between signing his "love Dads." He hadn't seen or heard Nathan fading in and out of a fitful sleep at his desk. The beige cubicle walls had hidden him. Nathan dreamed of candles and blood... of his dead father. It had only been a day and he was still struggling to come to grips with his father's passing.

Now some forty-five minutes after Bill's cumbersome departure, Nathan woke. Reality cut through the haze in Nathan's mind. The severity of his solitude crashed down upon him. All alone in the office, he felt like a trespasser. Mixed feelings of fear and being out of place. His forehead was sweaty, his mouth was dry. He had no gifts to give or cards to sign. He had no real reason for being there that late at all. Despite the longing and pain he felt, he knew his past had isolated him from his family. He missed his dad, or at least he thought he did. He was never good at relationships; an aspect of his personality his almost-fiancé could attest to. The thought of Alice and the pressure of her expectations shot him out of his chair and to his feet. He walked to the wall of the firm which was an expanse of glass. He rested his forehead against the office's wall of cold-tinted glass, his clenched fists pressed down on the chrome railing. He stared at his reflection for a moment.

He assessed the man in the glass; dark black hair, strong jaw, a little pale, but still a good-looking guy in his mid-to–late-twenties. He certainly looked the part, but he found no reassurance in his appearance. His head was swimming. His father, the guy who started it all, was gone. He never really relied on his dad for direction or advice, but with him gone, he missed having the option of reaching out to him. Especially since Nathan had chosen to follow in his footsteps. He closed his eyes. The glare of the city below chased the shadows in his head. The darkness comforted him.

Comfort was only momentary as his senses were assaulted by the halogen radiance that had instantaneously filled the office. Nathan spun to see who had come into the office. His quick glance around the cubicle wall caught the back of a gray dress and apron as it disappeared into Bill's cubicle. The cleaning crew was left with the remnants of Bill's gift preparations. His desk was closest to the elevator entrance, this location was a privilege reserved for the most senior members at Pendulum Accounting. Nathan's desk was farthest from the door and at times the long walk to the elevator intimidated him. Every time he needed to take a piss or grab a cup of coffee, he had to pass in front of fourteen senior accountants. No matter how hard he tried to ignore it, he could still feel their glances peering above their monitors assessing him, taking stock of Charley's boy and his progress without even speaking to him. Moving to Manhattan was hard for him, as was taking a job with a firm that knew his family name. He was a Cross and so he had a legacy of phenomenal success to live up to. He wondered with his dad being gone if any of that mattered anymore.

Nathan sat back in his chair, kicked his heels onto his desk, and feigned normalcy. An unidentified anticipation swelled inside him. Somehow interaction with another human being at that moment seemed dreadful. He quietly counted the moments before the cleaning lady would pass. His dream of his Father's tragic end had left him uncomfortable and uneasy. He could hear the plastic wheels along the floor. As the cleaning cart approached, he could hear the rise and fall of each of her footsteps. He laced his fingers behind his head and stretched, closing his eyes. He heard the cart stop next to him.

"Someone is missing you?"

Nathan opened his eyes to see a young woman with long black hair in a ponytail. Her skin was fair. Her accent was Czech, or maybe Polish. Her eyes were ice blue and mesmerizing. He unlocked his hands from behind his head. He pushed himself back from the desk and pulled himself into a sitting position. He squirmed and

11

Thrall

looked at his shoes. He bit his lower lip as he prepared to make eye contact with her again.

"Most likely…" he muttered.

His fingers teased with the lip of the drawer. He slowly opened and closed it. His gaze, like a child caught stealing, became fixed on her stare. Her hands were set on her hips like she was about to scold him.

"You've got no one to go home to tonight?"

GAVIN CROSS

Gavin wasn't at work when the call about his dad came in. He should have been at work, but he wasn't. He was home alone when he heard, nursing yet another hangover. He had been out of work for a couple of days now and was probably really close to being fired. Work at a paper mill is just that; work. Sweaty and back-breaking work. He had taken the job when he finished high school and stayed on out of comfort and lack of ambition. He didn't like his job, his boss, or his life. He never really needed to work. His family had money. His father's mid-life crisis had made the family very rich, filthy rich. His dad had been in accounting for twenty years and one day decided that the stock market was calling his name and within a year was a multi-millionaire.

Gavin had gone to live with his grandma when he was twelve. His brother Nathan had already gone off to boarding school by then. Nathan did everything he could to follow in his father's footsteps. Gavin was sure his father's death had hit Nathan the hardest. Charles Cross was more of an idea of a father than an actual father to both of them. Despite being absent for most of their young lives, Nathan always idolized his Dad; Gavin did too. Until their mom passed away, when their mother died everything had changed.

Gavin noticed how intensely hot it had gotten as he looked out the kitchen window of his Grandma's place. For as long as he could remember she had an outdoor thermometer on an angled bracket so that she could look out and decide if it was a day for gardening or not. The red cardinal in its center was now faded to a chipped and defeated pinkish purple. His Grandma had always loved cardinals and never missed an opportunity to add one somewhere in or around the house. He peered for what seemed like the first time in years out into the backyard through red-and-white-checkered curtains. The curtains still held onto the smell of his Grandma's fried chicken. Her famous brown bag recipe, with flour, Hungarian hot paprika, and black pepper. It was simple and delicious. His father had always loved her fried chicken and would beg for it whenever he visited.

Gavin remembered the days when he and Nathan, their mother and Grandmother would clear the dishes after dinner. Grandma hardly had anyone to cook for after Grampa died. She enjoyed it despite the work. She would curl her mouse gray hair up into a bun, her apron strings straining against her wide hips as they swayed between rinses while Mom washed. Her untrained voice would conjure a misplaced Gospel, a jumble of all the church tunes in her head, and leave it suspended in the air for everyone to try and join in. It always soothed everyone and made them feel at ease, especially Gavin's Dad.

Gavin remembered how Grandma would tuck Nathan and

him in as she whispered all she knew of "Amazing Grace." He couldn't think of a kinder person on Earth, and missed her more than words could say.

He let the curtain fall back into place before the tears came, and walked over the worn seventy's yellow linoleum and down the hallway. As Gavin passed the family collage on the wall, scattered portraits and photos in frames of the family smiled back at him. The expression seemed now to be a mockery of better times. A bright square where the sun hadn't faded the walls glared at him. This was the only picture he had taken down. His and Linda's Christmas engagement photo, taken at Sears and mass-produced as gifts for the family. Grandma had always been a picture bug and had to have the whole family on the wall. Gavin felt he had to keep them on the wall with her gone. Well, most of them anyway. She would have wanted it that way. Yet he couldn't bear to see the engagement photo day in and day out. The pictures led him to the bedroom. His eyes still hadn't stopped seeing his bed as half empty. Days like today it seemed altogether empty. He slid open the closet door and grabbed an old pair of Levi's jeans off the top shelf and a Budweiser T-shirt from the dresser drawer. It was worn so thin it was nearly transparent. Gavin thought that it would be light and cool in the heat. He slipped the jeans on and pulled the shirt over his head.

The blinking red light from the answering machine caught his eye. Finger poised on the gray sliding bar, he hesitated, and then slowly clicked it into the play position.

ANTIQUUS LIBELLUS
SERVATOR JOHN THOMAS

As I was instructed by Bobby Hayes, my predecessor, I have transcribed the contents of the Antiquus Libellus. The contents have reaffirmed my suspicions in regard to my sister's (Maggie Cross) unfortunate death and the circumstances surrounding the events which caused her demise.

It seems fitting to mention Bobby as he would never do so himself. He has passed the title of Servator to me as he has reached a point where "he is ready to walk into twilight," as he refers to passing on.

Bobby is part Lumberjack and part Abenaki, and he has always enjoyed his smokes and it has caught up with him in the end. So as his lung cancer progressed, he involved me more in the duties of being a Servator and how to track and identify the Gläm and their chattel.

Bobby is a good man and deserves to be remembered as such.

The reason I took over for him is due to what I started to piece together after Maggie's death. Maggie Cross (Thomas) was also a good woman, mother, and sister. She didn't deserve the hand she was dealt. She definitely deserved better than

Charles Cross; even with all his money he couldn't take care of her. Now I know that he planned on using her in ways that are unfitting for any person. She must have sniffed him out at some point and he had her done in. I would have killed him myself, but they will take care of that in the end. I still have a chance to set things right before all is said and done.

The Gläm are evil right to their core. They're the worst kind of bad in that it's just how they're made. They're wired to do harm. Unlike any man or woman who may do bad things to one another, these things operate on a whole different level. They feel no remorse, have no conscience, they do harm to people because that's what they are meant to do. It is all they have ever done. It is a matter of animal instinct, they feed on us and the pain and misery they inflict is just the icing on the cake.

I ripped one out of a guy who was actually feeding on his pregnant wife. I had a buddy at the State University take a look at it for me. He thought I was nuts. Granted I was paranoid, you never know who they've gotten to. I checked him out, his eyes were normal, and he had no tattoos or markings to show he'd been claimed. I explained how I came to discover them through the loss of my sister which I think helped him to at least see me sympathetically instead of just crazy.

After the initial shock when I dumped the thing on one of the tables in his lab, he got to work trying to figure out how they worked.

I am no scientist. Until now I had only heard them explained through myths and legends. Bobby said he heard them called Wendigos as a kid. The accounts of the Gläm were stories told to little kids to keep them in line and to keep them from running off in the night. Bobby said that when he did some asking around with some of the Old-timers they told him that the Vikings knew of them when they visited North America. He even was told that they worked together to

17

dispatch some of them.

The Vikings called them Ven. The first inhabitants of our country called them Wendigo. But most often they're known as the Gläm.

My buddy from the university could only speculate on how they came about, but from what I could understand they're old. Like from the beginning old, Old Testament old. There are references that the only things that the Leviathan feared were the Kilbit, creatures that clung to and killed their hosts. In knowing how they operate it sounds like just another name for the Gläm.

His findings were something along these lines. He has sworn to keep all of his findings secret and I trust him to do so. I hope that this will help Servators in the future to end all this. Perhaps science can find a way to rid the world of them.

He thought that it must have started with a virus, a virus that came out of the Earth itself. At the bottom of the ocean, vents spew out all manner of things, but he mentioned one thing called Archaea. That it somehow got infected and then ended up in some tube worms. These tube worms went from eating stuff that floated up from below to implanting themselves into whatever swam by and using them like a puppet or a vehicle much like a fish louse. Once they used up their host what popped out was a new version of whatever creature they lived in. So, this process went on and on until they made their way onto land.

HONEYSUCKLE

Gavin's hand shook a little. He had had nothing but bad news as of late from this damn thing. The robotic voice from the machine announced the day and time of the call:

Sunday, 9:48 AM

"Hey Gav, it's me," Phlip, one of his coworkers. "The boys and I missed you last night at the Shady Lady Lounge. Mr. Dobbins asked if I knew what was up with you missing work on Friday. I told him I didn't know. Don't forget bowling and brews tonight at the Sundowner, see ya."

Gavin ran his hand over his head and moved down the hall to the front door. As he swung open the screen door, the aluminum smashed against the side of the brick ranch. The door left a chalky white smear. He kept forgetting to get a new chain for it. The sound must have startled young Billy Rutherford. The boy half spun half jumped around to look at Gavin. He stared as if he was looking at an apparition. He stopped in his tracks along the road.

"Hiya, Gavin. Howyadoin'?" His adolescent fear of saying the wrong thing was betrayed in his wavering voice.

"Fine, thanks, how about you?" Gavin read in him that he was aware of what had happened. News travels fast in small towns.

"Sure is nice to see people at the house again, hated to see it empty."

"Ah, well I'm gonna get to work on the backyard, see ya."

"Oh, okay, I thought that… well the mill… and all." Billy struggled to find the words. Gavin rescued them both.

"I'm takin' some time, ya know, with Dad's passin'."

"My folks and I are real sorry to hear about it."

"Hey, tell your folks I send my best. I got to stop fartin' around and clean up that mess." Gavin gestured to the backyard. "Take care, Billy."

"See ya around, Gav." Billy turned and walked down the road towards his house, towards Linda's old house. She and the Rutherfords were neighbors back in the day. Gavin watched him until he disappeared from view behind the tree line. The heat hit him quickly. The humidity of the late August day settled instantly on his arms and brow. Droplets of sweat rapidly turned to streams and ran down his back and chest as he weeded. Sweat began to collect in his eyebrows and trickled into his eyes before he could stop pulling up jewelweed shoots and wipe them away. The heat was oppressive, but he needed to do something. He needed to be engaged physically to keep his mind off the heaping mound of loss he had been served over the last two years. He didn't want to think about Mom, Linda, Grandma, or now Dad. What they said had happened to Dad, *God*, he thought, *how does something like that happen?*

The extreme heat constantly reminded him of how much harder the work was, harder than it needed to be. It afforded him a silent kind of pissed-off pity party. He had sworn to himself to keep up his Grandma's place. When Linda left he couldn't have cared less about the yard, the dishes, or anything that resembled upkeep. He knew with everything that had happened, Grandma would understand. She had always prided herself on her flowers: lilacs, cannas, roses, and her honeysuckle bush that sat in the far right back corner of her property. She used to say it was "wild but under control." It served as a border of sorts between the woods beyond the house and the yard.

The only rest from the heat was an occasional breeze. The wind would loll across the lawn and lap at his soaked shirt. It continued up into the uppermost branches of the pines that separated their property from Mr. Rutherford's, the green needles swaying from their original position ever so slightly. Each breeze reminded Gavin to wipe his brow and determined him to keep at the task at hand. The black-handled clippers twisted in his sweaty hands. The blades opened and closed on one low-lying intruder after another until he had freed what remained of Grandma's flower garden. As he finished, he was rewarded with a breeze, and as it passed he followed it with his eyes to the badly overrun honeysuckle.

Honeysuckle was a common plant in these parts it grew on

roadsides and abandoned lots. His Grandpa had warned him of its allure. He had said the Old-timers used it for perfume since they were so poor. Gavin was feeling that allure; the heat had wrung out the scent and compelled him to rescue the flowers being strangled. It was a source of memories from long dead times, times he thought were better left dead. He remembered a moonlit walk hand-in-hand with Linda. His first kiss beneath the stars and years later that sweet smell on their skin, petals in their hair as they made love beneath it.

ANTIQUUS LIBELLUS
SERVATOR JOHN THOMAS

Transcribing all of the entries from the other Servators puts one of the first encounters as far back as ancient Egypt. It's impossible to know exactly how far back these things go. The first recorded encounter dates back to Egypt, but who can say whether or not other, more primitive people, succumbed to them? It must have taken a long time, body-hopping from host to host, to make it from the depths of the sea to land. The earliest entries refer to the madness during Akhenaton's reign. Egypt depended on the Nile's cycles of flooding to ensure the irrigation of crops. It seems that the Gläm have used waterways as a means of transportation for quite some time. The other aspect that seems to be involved with their presence is the flourishing of society. Historically the Gläm have infiltrated societies via waterways, but more importantly, these societies have grown in size and power. I've been trying to figure out what determines which society they go after. Surely every place could be accessed by water in some way. I think the factor that lures them in is power. More specifically the lust for power. Somehow power-hungry people are like a beacon for them or perhaps they are the easiest targets for manipulation. But, as was the case in ancient Egypt, those who craved power formed a pact with the Gläm.

I think that part of the reason I'm summarizing so much of this is because of the timetable of my plan. I don't think I will be able to just watch things go on. Those who served before me were able to be patient. They only acted when the time was right. My fear is that in our modern times, we have already missed that moment. It may be too late. As a result of Charles' death, I am taking a far more direct approach, which may ultimately require that my successor be brought up to speed rather quickly.

Getting back to Egypt, Akhenaton sought to funnel even more power into the already powerful role of Pharaoh by changing the religion of the people from a polytheistic faith to a monotheistic one in which he was the central figure. Apparently, he killed his own brother to secure the throne and once in power, he began to make drastic changes. These changes were a result of the Gläms' influence and ultimately would work to achieve their goals in the end, not the aspirations of Akhenaton. Unfortunately, one of the goals of the Gläm is to create a suitable habitat for themselves. The other factor of the Gläms' success is that humanity would be relegated to cattle, serving them and being served as sustenance to them. Akhenaton's plans were undone, by one of the head priests whose power he was trying to subvert. As a result, the original Antiquus Libellus was scribed by the first Servator, an Ancient Egyptian Priest.

A Persian sailor was the next to take on the role of Servator as Persia became infected by the Gläm's presence. The journal entries are inconclusive as to whether or not the Gläm were transported from Egypt or sprang up from somewhere else. The amount of time the Persian people spent on the sea would make them a likely target, especially during their attempts at conquest. Xerxes put down a rebellion in Egypt which may have been the remnants of the Gläms' forces being run out of town, at which point the Gläm may have been given the opportunity to strike a pact with Xerxes.

The way in which the Gläm actually spring up is difficult to determine as they reproduce asexually through some sort of binary fission. They truly behave like an intelligent and opportunistic virus. The Persian Servator was able to recruit a Greek student of philosophy during the siege of Athens. The Persian had seized an opportunity to turn the tides in Athens but was mortally wounded in the process. The Gläm are formidable but are vulnerable, especially while living in their hosts. So, in essence, if you kill their host they will die.

The Persian was able to trap them while they met secretly in the night. Often times what would have been perceived as decadent orgies were orchestrated buffets meant for feeding. According to the accounts of the journal he burned the entire structure, killing them. Yet the Gläm are all connected by a hive mentality, so as they perished the others were made aware and escaped persecution. The Persian forces were thwarted and the Antiquus Libellus changed hands next in Rome.

ALLURA

Nathan's hands shifted from the lip of his drawer to the arms of his chair. He shifted himself to one side with childlike nervousness. He did have someone waiting for him, well sort of. His soon-to-be fiancé, soon-to-be roommate, and lately estranged girlfriend, Alice, was waiting for his call. He hadn't had the guts to commit, and his father's death was another means by which he could avoid doing so. He still enjoyed his romps with the boys and was having a hard time wrapping his head around the concepts of responsibility and monogamy.

Shifting to the other side of his chair, he tilted his head to one side and asked, "Is that a proposition?"

He couldn't believe he had just uttered those words. Before he could formulate an internal response, she replied, "Interested?"

His eyes widened, his jaw dropped, and he stumbled for a response.

She intervened, "I'm Allura. I am going to meet some friends for drinks when I'm done."

Could this be happening? This kind of thing doesn't happen. Nathan's brain was spinning. First off, where did he get the balls to come right out and ask? He also wondered since when did drop-dead gorgeous girls join the cleaning crew. Was he imagining it or did her accent diminish as well? Either way, this was the chance of a lifetime and an excellent distraction.

"That sounds great! I just need to finish up a few things here and I'll meet you at the elevator. Oh… Sorry. My name's Nathan." He could feel his cheeks blush.

"I know." She arched an eyebrow at him, confused.

"Really, have we met before?" He wondered.

"No, it says so on your desk." She smiled "I'll be done in fifteen minutes, a few more trashcans to dump. I'll meet you then." She turned the cart around and headed towards the exit.

"Great." Nathan was beaming. Now came the hard part, lying to Alice. He drummed his fingers on the desk, his cell phone inches from his hand. He flipped it open hastily and let out a sigh. Alice was on speed dial. He pressed the number two and send. Alice answered before the first ring finished.

"Nathan?"

"Yeah, honey, it's me." He pretended to sound exhausted. "I'm not coming over tonight."

"Is everything alright?" Alice's concern was sincere and Nathan knew it.

"Yup, I'm just beat. I can't seem to get anything done all day. I stay late and just stare at the monitor." Nathan was purposefully pulling at her heartstrings. "I need to get my head straight before I get

27

myself canned."

"Honey," Alice yawned. "I'm sure they understand. It hit them too, your Dad was a partner in the firm. You haven't taken any time yourself to deal with losing him."

She was right but Nathan wasn't looking for sympathy. He just needed to cover his ass. At least she bought his story.

"You're right, you're right. I'm headed to bed; sorry I woke you."

"It's okay I was worried when I didn't hear from you. Love you."

"Me too." He couldn't bring himself to say it under the circumstances. He hoped she wouldn't notice.

"Night." Alice sounded half asleep already.

"Night, honey."

Nathan closed the phone and turned off his desktop. He switched off his lamp and headed down the corridor toward the elevator. He swung his blazer over his shoulder with one hand and out of the corner of his eye noticed the scraps of wrapping paper on Bill's desk and floor. It simply registered as odd.

The lights were off in the hallway and the large glass doors of Pendulum Accounting were etched with the firm's name and logo. He could barely make out the two women in front of the elevators. As he got closer, he recognized Allura. She and another woman were standing in front of the elevator. Their faces and torsos were faintly illuminated by the semi-circle of amber Roman numerals above the elevator doors. Allura was handing her a stack of clothes that looked like the uniform she was wearing earlier. There was also an envelope on top of the folded garments. Allura handed them to the woman. The woman in the cleaning uniform nodded; well, more like bowed to her as she took the uniform and envelope. Allura saw him coming as did the cleaning lady. She turned quickly and disappeared into the supply closet.

Nathan was surprised to see that Allura had changed into a simple yet elegant black evening dress which accentuated all of her womanly glory. It was low cut on top and high cut at the bottom. She wore black stockings, no jewelry, and tall patent leather stilettos. She was tall and curvy, built more like a tennis player than a bikini model.

"Nathan," she called to him as he passed through the glass doors. She stretched out one hand in a somewhat Victorian fashion. He quick-stepped to take it and noticed a black tribal tattoo of sorts wrapping around her wrist. Just as he had taken her hand the elevator doors opened.

Nathan was flabbergasted when he saw Allura's friends were waiting in the elevator. Two women similarly clad in black dresses, with bright blue eyes and pale skin waited inside.

"Nathan, let me introduce you to my dear friends, Cleo and Paige."

She waved her hand like Vanna White gesturing to the women in the elevator. They nodded silently.

"Ladies, Nathan," she gestured to Nathan. "Nathan, Ladies."

"Delighted," Nathan strained to sound suave.

Allura smiled. "Now that introductions are out the way." She wrapped her arm in Nathan's and led him into the elevator. "Let the fun begin."

DAYDREAM

It troubled Gavin that such a sweet memory would hurt so much. His first time with Linda felt so right when he was a kid. They had been together since she was twelve and he was twelve and three-quarters. They met when he went to live with his Grandma. He remembered the first time they adventured to Mr. Rutherford's old, dilapidated barn out behind that very same honeysuckle bush. She was always curious. Even as a grown woman, she would ask "Gav honey" this and "Gav honey" that. That same curiosity led them to the Rutherford's barn when they were sixteen or so.

The two of them snuck behind it, avoiding the front entrance. The barn's slats were worn gray planks rough cut from the Mill. The nails holding it together bled rust down from their lodgings. Once inside they inspected the tractor and tools. Linda climbed onto the seat and stood up on it like Superman above Gavin's head. She leaned one arm triumphantly forward in a fist and fell into Gavin's arms. She stared up at him and quick as lightning snuck a kiss. Gavin looked down at her in adoration and then gave a long and gentle kiss.

Years later, they walked that same path. They went for a walk almost every night after dinner. They would meet at the honeysuckle and walk hand-in-hand. The moonlight set her strawberry blonde halo ablaze. Her wings were his all-too-large flannel, the red and green sleeves cutting the air with every twirl. He was drawn to her sense of wonder and innocence which were evident in her whirling way of walking. She turned to him as they reached their meeting place; her eyes begged him, her breath warm and sweet on his face. Forever that smell would remind him of that night beneath the moon and honeysuckle. Now she was gone.

Now Gavin was alone and couldn't get his head straight. He was in trouble at work, didn't get to see his daughter, and he was being forced to see a therapist.

He closed his eyes. The smell of the honeysuckle still haunted him. He tried to imagine a more endearing past, a past that would allow him to accept just how low life had left him. All the money in the world didn't matter. What could he do with it? Money couldn't make things right; it couldn't bring back his father or patch things up with Linda. His drinking and distant behavior had pushed her too far. Events from his childhood haunted him even more now that he had a child of his own.

He went back to snipping dead branches and pulling weeds. As he did, he began to create in his mind a different story for his life, one that would make him a tragic hero. He deluded himself, another reason for him to visit his therapist, Dr. Larson.

Thrall

According to the good doctor and Linda, these delusions were Gavin's way of dealing with pain. He had a lot of loss in his life early on. Gavin saw these escapes from reality more as repressed memories, wild imaginings, and sometimes prophecy.

Gavin thought about Nathan living the good life in the city. He thought about Linda, little Clara, his baby girl, and Dad. He imagined them all together in the city. They had seen a matinee. He could smell the popcorn his father and Clara were sharing as they walked hand in hand lost in conversation. All of them were too preoccupied to see the men running towards them. One of them had on a hooded sweatshirt; it flailed behind him like a failed parachute. A barrage of bullets flew from a pale blue Honda. Gavin could hear them in his mind. Everything went into slow motion as the two young men were cut down. The ends of Linda's hair snapped her backward to the sidewalk, Dad crumbled in a heap overtop Clara. The contents of her purse were strewn across the city floor, lipstick, Juicy Fruit, keys, and a pink pacifier were mixed and mingled with popcorn and blood. The wind made Linda's curls writhe and twist on the ground as a leaf tumbled across the face of his angel.

It all became so vivid to him. He would go home to his all-too-small studio apartment every night. He would eat alone. He'd lay awake in bed, dreaming of the bastard who stole everything from him.

Gavin was snapped out of his twisted fantasy. He had taken a sizable chunk out of his thumb knuckle with his pruning shears. The gash was just big enough that the sweat made it sting. Shaking his head, he realized how wrong it was to murder off his loved ones.

Even if it was his way of making it easier to accept their absence, it was still deranged. The fact did remain that his father was murdered and someone would answer for that. His wife and daughter were still very much alive, off limits, but alive. This type of thinking had led to their distance. As of late, he had been moody, his emotions swinging from tears to rage for no apparent reason. He knew the only way to be close to them again was by way of Dr. Larson giving him his seal of approval. Gavin resolved to see the doctor as soon as he could. He took a moment to regard his day's work. Grandma would be happy. He salvaged her honeysuckle and stirred up a bunch of old memories in the process. He decided to head in for the day and tend to his wounds, both physical and otherwise.

A shower still afforded him some relief, a common but still effective home remedy. He brushed his teeth while drying his hair. He slid his toothbrush into a burnt orange Tupperware cup when he finished. It rattled around with Linda's old one, lipstick still smeared around its head. He dressed his thumb in the only band-aids he could find, Dora the Explorer, left behind by Clara. He didn't like what he saw in the mirror, circles under his eyes and a few days of stubble left him looking a bit too much like he felt.

After a commercial interrupted a colorized version of "She Wore a Yellow Ribbon," and a few too many Miller Lites, Gavin slid between the cool crisp sheets of his bed. He stared at the ceiling fan, the memories and fantasies of the day spinning around in his head like a tilt-a-whirl. He was snoring in minutes, and he slept solidly for the first time in many days. He never saw the moon setting the honeysuckle

Thrall

ablaze. He never heard the phone ring. The sound of Linda's voice woke him. He listened as she left a message.

"Gav honey, it's me. Clara hasn't spoken to you in two weeks. She misses you. The checks haven't come either. Call me."

Gavin rolled over in bed and sat up. He reached for the phone and plopped it between his legs, then grabbed a business card from the nightstand and dialed the number on the back. An answering machine picked up. It was a woman's voice, his receptionist, sounding like she was from Jersey.

"Dr. Larson's office hours are from eight to three, Monday through Friday. The office is currently closed. Please leave a message after the tone and someone in the office will get back to you as soon as possible. If this is an emergency, please hang up and dial 9-1-1."

Gavin waited for the beep, "Uh, hello Dr. Larson, this is Gavin Cross. I just wanted to leave you a message. I would like to see you as soon as you have an opening. Thanks."

CLUB DECADENCE

As the elevator descended, Nathan's guilt vanished. He really couldn't believe that he was about to tip back a few overpriced martinis with three hot Euro-babes. There was an instrumental version of Michele, by the Beatles playing. The three women were silent but smiling as if satisfied. *A good sign*, Nathan thought. As they reached the ground floor the lights were out. It was only illuminated by the lights from the street. A driver was waiting for them as they exited the building.

"You ladies roll in style," Nathan commented.

A tall well-built man in his mid-forties held open the door to an all-black sedan with tinted windows. He was silent. Allura sat in front with the driver. They spoke a few quick words in a language Nathan couldn't quite make out. He assumed it was Polish or maybe Russian. Cleo and Paige nestled in on either side of Nathan. They still smiled silently at him even though they were practically right on top of him. Like Allura, the women wore no make-up or jewelry. They had similar tattoos on their wrist, a sort of black tribal design. *Sorority sisters*, he thought to himself.

From the window, Nathan could discern they were heading into Lower Manhattan. The car was new; it still had that new car scent. Nathan noticed that the seat belts still had their packing plastic wrapped around their heads and that all of the burl wood accents were still protected by thin clear strips.

Allura turned around in front to speak with them. Her full profile came through in flashes and waves as headlights and streetlights lit up her face. She annunciated with a partially raised voice. "We're heading to our favorite club," she paused making sure she could be heard. "It's in the Meat Packing District, very exclusive, only open when the owner feels like it. We'll be there shortly."

She turned to face forward again. Nathan began to wonder how a cleaning lady had so many connections. As he was about to ask, Cleo's hand rested on his knee.

"I'm curious…" he began to ask.

Her hand slid to his inner mid-thigh. He looked at her; she smiled and pecked him on the cheek. He looked forward, stunned, and met eyes with the driver in the rearview mirror. The driver's glance made it clear to Nathan that he should keep quiet. His question remained unasked.

They slowed on Little West Twelfth Street and turned down a narrow lane that ended at what appeared to be a loading dock. A line of people, nearly sixty yards long, led to the entrance. The driver let the car crawl forward between the brick buildings. Nathan looked out the window, this time to Paige's side. He could have sworn that the people in line were bowing or nodding as the car passed. Paige caught his glances and aggressively kissed him. Allura lashed out in her foreign tongue without looking back, "*L'mih Om*" and Paige flew back into her seat. The car stopped.

Two human roadblocks, arms crossed, stood at the stairs of the dock. They could have been twins; both were well over six feet tall, shiny shaven heads, and were dressed all in black. They both were wearing sunglasses despite it being dark out and also had earpieces in to communicate with someone inside. When the driver went around the front of the car to get the door for Allura they nodded to him in a "what's up" kind of way. When they saw Allura their heads bowed, like the cleaning woman and the people in line. Nathan noticed the gesture. He began to wonder if this was some kind of stunt if Allura was some super-rich tycoon's daughter, or nobility. She may have needed to shed all the formality and live like all the little people for a night. He wasn't sure what was going on. One thing was evident; Allura was more than she had led Nathan to believe.

One of the doormen and the driver opened both of the back doors. Paige and Cleo got out and Nathan followed Cleo assuming it was safer to trail her after the awkward kiss incident with Paige. Nevertheless, they both encircled their arms with his like before as he passed in front of the car. The doorman who opened the door for them led the way into the club. Nathan found it odd that there was no sign, no posters, and no graffiti. Most clubs had some neon atrocity outside. No one was loud, no loud music, and people weren't huddled in groups outside smoking. As they entered, he felt important. He had a driver tailing him and a bouncer leading the way, two hot girls in his arms and he was invited by a princess or something. The other door guy was busy with the clubgoers waiting in line. Nathan watched him as he passed, hoping to hear him deny someone or see if they tried to slip him some money. Nathan spotted that he wasn't even checking for I.D., he simply waved his hand in a come here motion, and as he did a young woman stepped forward, lowered her head, and swung her long hair to one side revealing a tattoo on the base of her neck like Allura's.

The bouncer asked, "To whom do you belong?"

"Thomas," she replied, never raising her head.

"Welcome. Thomas is in room three."

He checked off a name on the clipboard. Nathan was impressed by the cordial nature of the doorman; most bouncers in New York lacked such refinement.

Allura and her entourage traveled swiftly inside. They proceeded down a pitch-black hallway with a soft red light at the end. Nathan felt a little claustrophobic but Cleo gave his bicep a reassuring squeeze as they reached the end of the tunnel-like hallway. The whole place was a concrete rectangle. The bar, bistro tables, and minuscule dance floor occupied the first third. The remainder of the establishment was a corridor with rooms off of a long hallway. The bar was immediately to their left; a very round and very grim-looking bartender leaned both arms on the battered wooden counter in front of him. He resembled a bulldog protecting a bone. Nathan veered toward the bar.

"Finally, a drink" he quipped "Could I have a martini, dry?"

"No drinks!" The bartender's accent couldn't hide his irritation.

"Oh… I thought…" Nathan stammered.

"Bruce," Allura scolded, "Nathan is my guest."

"My apologies, Madame Allura, I had no idea. One dry martini, coming right up."

Bruce was practically shaking, sweat beaded his brow and his jowls were quivering. Whoever Allura was, she apparently was not to be messed with. Nathan's head swelled, *damn right you'll make my martini*, he thought. Nathan was puzzled about the dusty bottles behind the bar and the apparent lack of use. Yet his minor triumph overshadowed his concern.

Bruce handed him his drink and Allura began to lead him away from the bar. They passed through a room littered with mix-and-match overstuffed sofas; people reclined and sat on the arms watching him pass. It was dimly lit by candles scattered on low tables in front of the furniture. The place wasn't redecorated very well, it looked like what it was; an old meat packing joint with a bar thrown in and some sofas. Nothing much to look at, but the company was good as was the very strong Martini. The six of them maneuvered between sofas and rejoined the hallway which extended the length of the place. One hallway ran from the docks past the bar area down past a series of small rooms. The rooms were old meat lockers, the refrigeration system was disconnected but the place remained damp and cool, with a sort of dank smell to it. Each of the rooms were set up like the area adjacent to the bar; sofas, candles on low tables, yet each one had a number spray painted near its doorway. The number wasn't even applied with a stencil, just freehanded, red spray paint running down the white cinder block walls.

Nathan glanced into one room, room three. A man around Nathan's age. maybe a few years older, sat with his arms resting on the back of the sofa. The young woman from outside was straddling his lap her hands gripping the back of the sofa. *She didn't waste any time*, Nathan thought, his mind began to entertain his chances of a similar situation.

"This must be Thomas," Nathan muttered to himself. He guessed they must have passed six or so rooms each with a similar scenario playing itself out inside.

At the end of the hallway they came to a large room. Unlike the other rooms, this room felt cooler and was even more poorly lit. There were throw rugs along the floor, but no sofas; instead, there were pillows in clumps all over the floor. It had three high-backed chairs against its far wall with a man seated in the middle chair. Two women sat at his feet and six men in black suits, three at either side, stood with their hands clasped in front of their waists. They all wore earpieces.

Allura strode into the room like she was at her prom. The bouncer and driver took up positions at the entrance of the room. Paige and Cleo left Nathan to lounge on a nest of pillows. Allura walked directly to the seated figure.

He was tall by the look of him. It was hard to see any of his features in the poorly lit meat locker. Allura kneeled at his feet, head bowed down, he patted her head and she rose to her feet, turned, and motioned to Nathan to join them.

It's like a scene from The Godfather meets Dracula, Nathan thought, standing stock still for a moment, dumbfounded. He was walking towards him before he knew it as if his body moved before his brain could catch up. He reached out his hand to shake his mysterious benefactor's hand. The man's hands were huge and bony, all knuckles and sinew. Nathan's hand was nearly crushed. He gave an elongated nod as it seemed as though it were the custom.

Allura made the introductions. "Nathan Cross," she gestured with her hand in that same Vanna White fashion, "this is Xavier Thrallson, our most benevolent host."

"It's a pleasure to meet you, sir."

Nathan had a strange feeling he was being weighed and measured by his host. He still couldn't really make out Xavier's features, as the man sat in total darkness. Even when Nathan shook his hand and Xavier shifted forward, his face was still shadowed.

Xavier rolled his hand over on the arm of his chair motioning for Nathan to sit in the chair on his right. "Nathan, please sit, and relax. Can I refresh your drink?"

Nathan had forgotten about the drink in his hand. He downed it and sat beside him. Allura moved to sit on the opposite side of their host.

"That would be lovely," Nathan said.

One of the women at Xavier's feet sprang up and retrieved

Nathan's glass. She quickly disappeared in the direction of the bar. Nathan wondered if Bruce would give her as hard of a time as he had given him.

"Cross?" Xavier mused. "By chance are you related to Charles Cross?"

"He is my father... was my Father." Nathan became quiet.

"Yes, my condolences, the time to shuffle off this mortal coil comes for us all. Your father was an acquaintance of mine. He handled some investments for me when he left Pendulum."

"Really? Dad did pretty well for himself. He had never played the market before and whams a homer right out of the gate." Nathan worried his sports analogy would make him sound trite.

"Indeed, his efforts made my contingent very wealthy. That wealth has freed up a great deal more time for us to indulge ourselves. Our little nightlife spot here is just one of many indulgences. Hence its name, Club Decadence is a bit over the top perhaps as far as names go. Are you finding it to your liking?"

Nathan looked down to find another martini in his hand. The delivery girl sat at his feet. He couldn't shake the feeling that everyone was waiting for his response.

ANTIQUUS LIBELLUS
SERVATOR JOHN THOMAS

In Rome, as was the case in Egypt, the centralization of power was an indication of the Gläms' presence. The change from a republic to an empire combined with the appetites of the Roman people made Rome a prime target. Roman engineering provided a means by which the Gläm could travel. The vast aqueducts and waterways spread over the Roman Empire allowed easy access. The Gläm were, no doubt, drawn by the power-hungry and decadent nature of the people.

Once the book landed in Rome, the Servators gained their name and the number of Servators in Rome and Roman territories grew. The book was transcribed and was still kept in secret despite there being more books in circulation. One disadvantage of more books existing in different locations is that at this point in history, gaps in our knowledge of the Gläm and their activities become more widespread. What can be gathered from early entries in this edition of the Antiquus Libellus is that the Gläms' influence in and occupation of the Roman Empire is definite and swelled at various points in the Empire's history. The

Thrall

Gläm are instinctually aggressive and violent and the gladiatorial entertainment and debauchery of the times enticed their appetites. These tendencies were reinforced in Roman times and have not diminished at all since. The Gläm love violence, pain, lust, and many other ugly and depraved emotions. It remains unclear as to whether or not these emotions satiate a need in them or if they simply are amused by them. They exploit these human flaws to reach their ultimate goal of turning our Earth into a habitat more suitable to them.

The only needs they have are a host and food. Although they can feed on both men and women, they need female flesh in order to reproduce. Eventually, they will no longer require hosts if a habitat more conducive to their survival exists. After three extended periods of incubation, they emerge, appearing human-like, after appropriating considerable raw proteins and DNA, and thanks to their tube worm ancestors they can live for centuries.

The conquest of new areas provided transportation and a food source. The Gläm are extremely patient and opportunistic, so they rarely fail to seize opportunities to further their goals. One key factor is that they need time to reproduce, especially in large numbers. They are vulnerable as a group during their pre-expansion phase. It takes a fully developed Gläm to reproduce and a fully developed Gläm takes three cycles to emerge. In order to evolve they must feed and feeding makes their presence more evident. They need groups of people, especially women, and events guised in such a way as to not attract attention. They are exposed and vulnerable during feeding and cannot be disturbed. The fire in Athens was an attack on such an event.

The Gläms' numbers in Rome and Roman territories did not grow steadily but built up to population booms or mass hatchings which can be linked to various dark blemishes on the timeline of events. The various upheavals in the decline of Rome didn't seem to dissuade the Gläm in their endeavors. It would seem that another aspect of the Gläms' eerie instincts is that apparently, they have enough sense to jump ship when things look grim. They seized an opportunity to branch out into Constantinople and the obvious conclusion would be that many editions of the Antiquus Libellus were destroyed when the library was burned. A more specific concern is that versions of the book which offered untold migrations and observations of the Gläm from before the Fall of Rome through the Reign of Alexander have been lost. The degree of insight these may have provided can't be determined but must be considered an incalculable loss. I can't help but feel that in an already one-sided battle, the loss of such information is equivalent to weapons missing from our arsenal.

DR. LARSON

When Dr. Larson checked his voicemail, he had two messages. The first was from Gavin Cross.

"Uh, hello Dr. Larson, this is Gavin Cross. I just wanted to leave you a message. I would like to see you as soon as you have an opening. Thanks."

The second was from Detective Becker, S.S.P.D. regarding Gavin.

"Dr. Larson, this is Detective Becker. As you may be aware Charles Cross passed away two days ago under some peculiar circumstances. We are aware of patient confidentiality, yet we were wondering if you could answer some very basic questions regarding Gavin Cross. We have been made aware of some instances in his past that may be of interest to us and would like your opinion on these issues. If you could give us a call or swing by the station it would be greatly appreciated. Thank you and have a good day."

Dr Larson knew all too well which instances the Detective

was interested in. He had started seeing the Cross boy when his mother passed away. He continued seeing Gavin; it seemed to hit him harder than Nathan. Nathan was headed off to boarding school near the time of his mother's death and despite his loss, he stuck to the plan. Gavin stayed with his father for a while, until moving in with his Grandma. Charles Cross sent Gavin to live with Grandma after a dream, maybe a nightmare, one night that shook Gavin so badly he couldn't let it go, ever.

* * *

Gavin was little when he lost his mom. That was also when he went to live with his Grandma. He was twelve when he saw his father eating someone in his study. It must have been four in the morning. Gavin heard some commotion in the house, so he went to investigate. He peered down the hall and he could see his father's study light on. The light cut a stretched triangle across the hardwood floor. The door had been shut three-quarters of the way and the light within was making a break for it. Gavin could hear the shuffle of feet and bodies inside. He couldn't make out words but he could hear a clicking sound and heavy breathing. He crept to the door, wondering who could be in there with his dad.

He knelt in front of the door and slowly, gently pushed the door aside to get a better look. A young woman was sitting on his father's roll-top desk her dress hiked up around her waist. His father was at the edge of his seat, his hands on the girl's kneecaps. Gavin could see the top of his father's head moving. He appeared to be kissing the girl's inner thigh. Gavin kept quiet, watching intently. His father's head began to come into view as his kisses moved from the inner thigh to the top of the quadriceps. He heard a low clicking sound as his father spasmed while clutching the back of the woman's calves. His grip intensified as he froze in place.

That's when Gavin saw the blood. His father's eyes were rolled back in his head, white, all-white eyes like a shark. His mouth was wide open, overextended like his lower jaw was dislocated. A black head like a snake's or a toad's or something was in Dad's mouth, its shiny black eyes gleaming. It had a long strip of the girl's leg in its mouth like it was unraveling her. She wasn't even screaming. Her back was arched, her head back and eyes closed. Gavin didn't scream until it saw him. It stopped peeling the girl and made a sound like a cicada. Gavin screamed, his father's eyes went normal and the thing slid down into his throat. The girl stirred only a little and murmured "What's going on?" Her eyes were still closed and her words slurred. Charles bellowed "Gavin what are you doing out of bed?"

Gavin ran to the phone in the living room and dialed.

"9-1-1, what is your emergency?"

"My dad, he…"

Gavin heard the line click. He looked up to see his father had hung up the phone with his finger on the switch hook. He dropped the handset and ran like hell to his room. He dove under his bed skinning the back of his head and left shoulder. He could hear his father shouting.

"You've got to get the hell out of here!"

"What…" The woman from the study sounded drunk, "Come on just a little more."

Gavin heard a slap. Charles had smacked the woman across the face.

"Snap out of it. He dialed 9-1-1. You've got to go, now."

Gavin heard the woman rustling around gathering her things. She ran out the front door, started her car, and tore off. Gavin lay under the bed, panicked and afraid, hoping this was all a dream. The pain at the back of his head told him it was real. The warm sensation of blood spreading through his hair and trickling down the back of his neck made him feel squeamish. He waited there in silence for his father to come into his room. He never came. Eleven minutes later he could hear the sirens approaching. It was still dark out. He heard a car pull up, then another. Car doors slammed. The front door slammed.

"Sir, stay right there." An officer directed his father.

"Officer, I'm Charles Cross. I live here. My son called."

"Okay, well what's going on here?" The officer's voice had lost a bit of the edge it contained earlier.

"My son is very upset. He lost his mother, my wife, not too long ago. He stumbled in on me while I was… involved with a woman. I thought he was asleep. I'm afraid it was too much for him. He's hiding under his bed."

Gavin was listening. He heard every word. He was right, it was too much for him to handle. How did he know where he was? He hadn't ever come into the room.

"How old is the boy?"

"Twelve."

"Is he okay?"

"I really don't know, he won't come out or speak to me. I can understand. I don't know what I was thinking." Charles ran his hand over his head. "I should have never brought her here, to the house. I was lonely."

"Where is this woman now?" The edge in his voice returned.

"She took off, embarrassed. Would you like to come in?"

"Yes, I would like to talk to the boy."

Gavin heard the front door open. He heard footsteps.

"Where is the boy's room?"

"At the end of the hall…"

"Mr. Cross, I'd appreciate it if you stayed here in the living room while I spoke with the boy." Officer Madson started down the hall, stopped, and turned back to Charles. "What's his name?"

"Gavin."

He turned back down the hall and slowly opened Gavin's door. He flipped on the lights. He sat on the corner of the bed and spoke softly.

"Gavin, my name is Bill. I'm a police officer. I came here to check on you."

Gavin was silent, he didn't dare speak.

"Are you alright under there?" Something in the man's voice reassured Gavin. He sounded tough but sincere and caring.

"I hit my head when I slid under here." Gavin's voice was

shaking.

"How bad is it?"

"I think it's bleeding. I hit my shoulder too."

"There are paramedics waiting outside. I'll go and bring them into your room. Do you think you can come out once they are here?"

"Where's my dad?"

"He's waiting in the living room. I asked him to wait a bit."

"Don't let him in here!" Gavin shrieked.

"Okay but how about I go get my buddies out there to have a look at that noggin of yours?" The officer knelt down then got on his belly and peered under the bed. He lifted the sheet and comforter out of the way with his right hand, his weight on his left. He looked into Gavin's wide eyes.

"Does that sound okay?"

Gavin gulped back tears, "Okay, I'll come out when they come in."

"Okay, then." Madson pushed himself up on the side of the bed and left the room to get the paramedics. He walked down the hall and into the living room.

"Boy's pretty spooked. Wait here till we check him out."

"Oh, is he alright?"

"That's what I intend to find out sir. I'm going to get the guys to have a look at him." Madson opened the front door and waved in the paramedics.

After a fair amount of flashlight in the eyes and some cleaning of scrapes, the paramedics were on their way out the door and Madson and Gavin were alone together in the room. Gavin refused to make eye contact as he sat cross-legged on the floor beside his bed. Madson's son was only a few years younger and as such he knew what Gavin had in mind.

Madson took one knee and asked, "Are you gonna make a break for it?"

"Huh," Gavin responded without ever looking up. His fingers toyed absently with the hem on the leg of his pajama bottoms.

"What I meant to say was... are you going to dash back under the bed when I call your dad in here?" Madson's voice was more firm.

Gavin looked up at him his eyes pleading. "Please, I can't see him, It's not him. He's got a thing inside him. He was tearing that lady apart. She couldn't see, but I could, and he wasn't there. I mean his eyes weren't there. They were gone. I don't want to be here not with him. I can't. Please don't make me. Don't leave me here alone with him or he'll get me too. I..."

"Whoa," Madson cut him off. "Listen, buddy, your dad is out there and he's worried about you. He's waiting to hear that you are okay."

"That's not my dad. I don't know what he is but he's not my dad."

"I know you're real upset and all, but that is your dad. He was spending some time with a lady. I know she wasn't your mom but he's just lonely is all."

"My mom is dead." Gavin's statement was cold and steely

52

and left the room quiet.

Madson couldn't argue with that. He rubbed his face and stood up, hiking up his belt and revolver. He walked down the hall to Charles. Gavin could hear them.

"Mr. Cross, the boy is real upset and he is pretty scared. He's okay but he doesn't want to spend the night here. Is there anyone he could sleep over with for a night or two?"

"Ah, well my mother lives about twenty minutes away. I could drop him off, but I would have to call her. She's probably sleeping."

"Well, why don't you give her a call? I'll swing the boy over to her house. I'll have him pack up a few things."

Charles moved to dial the phone as Madson walked to Gavin's room. When Madson got to Gavin's door, he was waiting with a blue gym bag with red handles all packed and ready to go. Madson made an after you gesture and Gavin bolted through the house and out the door and stood beside the car.

Charles was standing there with the receiver in his hand and a puzzled look plastered on his face. Madson walked by and shook his head. The no connection sound snapped Charles out of it.

"He's okay?" Charles asked.

"He's moving pretty good." Madson paused searching for words. "I'll call you tomorrow with the number of someone for Gavin to talk to so he can straighten all this out in his head. You can set up an appointment for him."

"Oh, alright, well thank you for everything." Charles forced an awkward smile. "Everything will be alright Mr. Cross." Madson lied;

somehow he knew things wouldn't work out. Madson drove Gavin over to stay at his Grandma's that night. That was the last night Gavin ever spent with his dad. The next afternoon was Gavin's first of many visits to Dr. Larson.

* * *

"Hello, Detective Becker," Dr. Larson had his phone pinioned between his face and shoulder his hands flipping through his planner, "This is Dr. Larson returning your call."

"Dr. Larson, it's me, Madson. How are things?"

"Oh, things are going pretty well. I received Becker's call about the Cross boy. I probably shouldn't speak about it, but you've known him as long as I have. When it comes right down to it, he's delusional. When the world gives him lemons he makes lemonade, mixes in LSD, and off he goes."

"You think the boy is on drugs?" Madson had a defensive and questioning tinge in his voice.

"Oh no, not literally, I mean that when things get tough for him, he creates a version of reality that is easier to digest, albeit far out, but somehow easier. It's like a defense mechanism."

"Do you think he would hurt his father?"

"Off the record, I just don't know. Part of me says no way, but a part says dad is where this all started. So... maybe. He did just split with his wife and kid. Who knows?"

"Thanks, Doc. I really appreciate being able to just talk and sashay all the formality."

"It's my job." Dr Larson hung up the phone. He looked at his watch. 9:25. His receptionist buzzed him, "Your 9:30 is here."

Dr. Larson looked at his planner. His elbows were on his desk, his hands in fists holding up his head. His receptionist, Donna, had penciled in an appointment without letting him know. He hated that, especially when his 9:30 may have just heard a conversation about himself while sitting in the waiting room. A conversation that violated confidentiality and could cost Dr. Larson his livelihood and his license to practice. Dr. Larson pushed himself away from his desk, spun in his faux leather swivel chair, and popped up to his feet. He swung the door inwards and opened it, one hand on the doorknob the other waving Gavin into his office. "Come on in, Gav."

Gavin peeked up over a magazine and then slapped the magazine on the table beside him and scooted around Donna's desk. Donna was Dr. Larson's offensive line in a manner of speaking. Her desk prevented direct access to Dr. Larson's door as did her personality. She may not have been the most professional receptionist in the world but she was fierce and loyal. She could stall, scare, and butter up clients without missing a beat and oftentimes just by reading Dr. Larson's non-verbal cues. There was her decibel level and Jersey accent, gum chomping, and the odd tattoo on the ankle but she earned her keep.

Gavin was used to the routine. He walked over to the sofa and plopped down. He was enveloped in beige. The good doctor believed in comfort over style and his sofa, although dated, exuded comfort. As a matter of fact, many times Gavin had drifted off to sleep during their sessions. Today, Gavin was nowhere near sleep; he desperately needed to talk some things out. As he began to speak, Dr. Larson's phone went off indicating he had a text message.

"One sec, Gav." The doctor dug in his pants pocket for the phone. He flipped it open and read the message.

-We are confident the eldest son will accept. No need for younger. Please remedy.

Gavin began to speak but Dr. Larson flipped his phone shut and cut him off.

"Gav, in light of everything going on I want to try something radical. Are you up for a challenge?"

ANTIQUUS LIBELLUS

SERVATOR JOHN THOMAS

The rumors regarding Alexander the Greats' involvement with the Gläm fall on both sides of the fence. From what I read, the Servators were unsure of where his alignments were when it came right down to it. Some assumed that his conquests had to be a sure indicator of the Gläms' influence while others thought that his mass killings were an effort to eradicate the Gläm after having been informed of their presence by the oldest order of the Servators in Egypt. Any sure indicator of his allegiance was lost in the fires of Alexandria.

The Mongols were similarly categorized. Having such a landlocked empire would prohibit the Gläm, but not entirely eliminate them from the equation. Rumblings about various rulers throughout the time and their involvement appear in a speculative fashion but the next confirmed outbreaks come from the Vikings.

The Vikings referred to them as the Wen or Ven. The proud and fierce nature of the Norse people only adds to the level of severity in their tales. One can only assume that for them to live in fear of anything it must have indeed been a menace. When the outbreak of the Gläm became intensified during an especially brutal winter whole villages were nearly decimated. The survivors adopted a slash-and-burn policy. They were able to escape the members of their ranks who'd been under the Gläm's possession. Yet an unforeseen variable was that those who were left to the elements would inevitably freeze. The frozen corpses were set adrift at sea. One such body was discovered off the coast of North America by Vikings while they were en route to trade with Native Americans in the northeast. The frozen body must have been near death and unconscious. He would have been placed in a skiff or raft and set ablaze. When they attempted to give their fallen comrade a traditional burial, they unthawed a ravenous Gläm and set it loose in North America. The Ven attacked one of its fellow Vikings, most likely vomiting the Gläm into one of them by force given its desperate circumstances. These odd conditions would allow the Gläm to prey upon the early inhabitants of the continent.

The Wendigo myth of a cannibal who converts those it feeds upon, persists through colonial days. The myth of the Skin Walker is similar as well but is geographically removed from the eastern portion of the continent.

Another foggy area of Gläm influence occurred during the Age of Exploration. My mentor, Bobby, seems to be very certain of the Gläm's effect on Mesoamerica. He states that there are too many indicators of the Gläm's presence at Tenochtitlan to be coincidental. The great city was terraformed on a lake and provided easy access. The civilization's rise to power ending in a mysterious and bloody decline is a strong indicator. The images and myths of gods wearing human and animal skins as well as Quetzalcoatl, the feathered serpent resembling a Gläm, also seem suspect. Yet the gray area seems to be if the Conquistadors spread the Gläm to Europe and the Americas or if they found their own way. Surely enough

European groups were present in the continent for traffic to flow either way. Yet it would seem as though during the Age of Impressment the Gläm, with their patient foresight, had big plans afoot.

Scores of men were swept away from bars and alleyways and taken out to sea aboard many sea-going vessels. It was from one of these men that a Servator was told of the plans of the Gläm to pull more of their kind from the deeps. He had been impressed into service and came to consciousness aboard a ship outside of Portsmouth. He was bound but his gag had fallen out of place during his struggle. He woke to the scream of one of the others. The man next to him was screaming as he witnessed one of the Gläm setting in to devour one of the other inmates. He himself screamed when he realized what was afoot, startling one of his captors. His tormentors kicked him in his guts for his disturbance and he rolled onto his side.

From there he noticed the pour soul on the other side next to him. He was already dead and had a knife on his hip. He waited until they went up deck to remove the knife and cut his ropes. He snuck up top to find them bringing up great nets of what looked like eels and transferring them with great care to huge barrels filled with water. He slipped overboard, unnoticed, and swam to shore. When he got ashore, he found a tavern to warm his bones beside the fire. He inquired around the tavern as to where the ship was headed. The barkeep told him, "South, somewhere called Roanoke."

TUNNELS

The discovery of the hidden passage had bewildered local law enforcement. It took a couple of days to get paperwork and officers organized to investigate the situation. The delay had infuriated Madson. He was tromping down the stairs so hard the single light bulb hanging overhead seemed to be jolted with each thud of his feet. The stairs were narrow and his frame filled the passage almost completely. Becker was in hot pursuit of him and they both stopped to collect themselves at the bottom of the stairs. In front of them was another door that led into the expanse of the basement. On their right were built-in shelves painted cream and loaded with bocce, badminton, croquet sets, coolers, and such. The two detectives seemed to share a common thought.

Madson uttered it first, "Rich guy's basement looks like mine so far."

"Mine too," Becker added.

Although both of them knew there was something different

about this basement, they wouldn't be here in the first place.

Most guys on the force knew their routine and would not have busted in on one of their sessions if it wasn't absolutely necessary. Madson reached for the knob, his hesitation noticed by Becker. He swung the door wide with one fast push. The door opened inwards and part of him was waiting for something to jump out at him. The little hairs on the back of his neck were standing at full mast. Yet there was no boogeyman poised to pounce, no blood-soaked walls within. Madson and Becker were greeted by a well-lit and tidy washer and driver with neatly kept shelves brimming with detergents and laundry supplies. The space was clean and ran in a long rectangle.

The concrete floors were painted a battleship gray, no doubt a sealer of some sort to keep moisture at bay. The place sat directly on the shelf of rock that ran below the city and beneath that layer of stone, springs carved their path across town to High Rock Park. The walls were lined with shelves and various bicycles, a canoe and very expensive sets of golf clubs leaned at intervals along the shelved walls. As far as basements go the only thing out of the ordinary was that everything was impeccably in order.

As they moved toward the end of the basement a small door was situated at the far right corner. Conversation and radio chatter could be heard beyond it and flashlights moved in sweeping arcs which were visible beneath the door. It seemed as though the halogen bulbs weren't working above the door. Madson reached up and twisted them without thinking. They sprang to life.

"Loose!" he quipped to Becker with a goofy sideways grin.

Becker responded in kind with a note of seriousness in his voice. "Why?"

Becker's response smoothed the expression on Madson's face quickly into a more somber and 'Oh shit… fingerprints' kind of expression. Madson reached apprehensively, once again, to turn the knob. Again, it opened inward and he clipped a fellow cop with the door. The young man in uniform nearly somersaulted into the hole in the rock wall, having been crouched like a catcher shining his flashlight down the hole for his partner. Madson wasn't a fan of tight places and the door led him to a broom closet with a dirt floor and racks of wine bottles on either side. The dirt floor sloped into a ledge of bluish-gray rock which acted as an oversized cornerstone of sorts for the foundation. The hole tilted downwards into the rock and the opening was roughly the size of a car door. Madson backed out of the doorway and motioned with his hand for Becker to take his place.

"Cramped." Madson huffed under his breath.

Becker nodded in affirmation, knowing full well what the matter was, and spoke to the officer remaining in the crude doorway.

"What do we got, Kenny?"

"Sir, we've got three guys down there each taking different tunnels. Each of them has said that there are strange markings on the stone walls. And believe it or not, there are steps."

"Steps?"

"Yes sir, someone made a solid set of steps out of pressure-treated lumber leading from here down into the tunnels." The officer's radio barked as one of the brave tunnel rats was checking in.

"Kenny, this is Johnson. Please respond."

"Go for Kenny. Johnson, what is your twenty?"

"You wouldn't believe it; I just came out near the Pavilion at High Rock Park just down from the Station."

"Near the Station?" Madson asked from beyond the door. "Could this day get any weirder?"

* * *

The Police department sits at a slant behind Town Hall just off Broadway on the side of the hill. Saratoga Springs' main drag is Broadway and it basically runs sideways between two hills, one slopes down from it heading west and one rises up from it heading east. Saratoga is often referred to as being at the foothills of the Adirondacks. This would explain the hilly aspect of the area but what runs beneath those hills brought people to the area in the first place. Springs drew people from far and wide. The healing properties of the springs were well-known to the Iroquois. The culprits behind Charles Cross' death were also well known to the Iroquois and have been making use of the natural tunnels for centuries.

"Kenny, this is Pierce. Please respond."

"Go for Kenny. Pierce, what is your twenty?"

"I'm not sure as of yet. There is some light ahead. Some bushes are blocking the way. Gimme a sec."

Madson, Becker, and Kenny waited for Pierce to speak. They listened intently for any sound, as might children late one Christmas

Thrall

Eve.

"I hear water. Bushes are pretty thick." A car horn honked in the distance. The sound startled the listeners. "Kenny, I'm in CongressPark. I'm looking at Spit and Spat."

Spit and Spat were spouting water at one another as they do every summer. Two plaster sculptures of twin Tritons sit spewing water through their conch shells. The elaborate fountain rests just below an Italian garden with statues of Satyrs and Maidens that has been newly recreated to its former glory. More importantly, the tunnel was adjacent to the Canfield Casino. The Casino sits smack dab in the middle of Congress Park, which is itself right in the middle of town.

Madson stared silently, astonished, into the opening in the wall. He turned, his mouth gaping, to his partner.

"Beck… What the hell is going on here?"

"I have a feeling that there is much more going on here than we realize."

"How many guys did you have in there Kenny?"

"Just three, sir."

"Who is the third?" Becker asked Kenny.

"Morgan, sir."

Madson's expression turned grave as he faced Kenny. The worry was apparent on his face.

"You haven't heard from him yet?"

"Not yet sir."

"Call him," Becker commanded.

"Morgan, what's your twenty?"

"No idea Kenny, but I'm sloshing through some kind of muck on the floor. As soon as I know, I'll let you know."

Madson looked from Becker to Kenny and down at the floor. He ran his hand over his head. He motioned to Becker to follow him and they headed back out to the car to confer alone.

"Sir?" Kenny spoke as they began to leave.

"What is it, Kenny?"

"I thought I should tell you..."

"What? What is it?" The frustration was evident in Becker's tone.

"Sir, each of the guys took one tunnel from the three just below the stairs." Kenny timidly offered his words.

"Yeah, so?"

"Well, sir they each also said there were at least three more."

"Each?" Becker asked puzzled.

"Yes, sir, each guy reported seeing three tunnels branching off from the ones they were following."

"That makes at least nine possible destinations," Becker added flatly.

Madson was hot at this recent news. He radioed dispatch angrily. "Dispatch. This is Madson. I need any available units at the Cross house with flashlights, ASAP."

"Copy, that Madson. They're already there."

In his huff, Madson had forgotten the throngs of uniformed wall flowers lurking about upstairs. It wasn't long before he heard footsteps. Becker gave verbal orders to check in every ten minutes and sent the men into the tunnels. Each was to take one of the branches off of the three main tunnels. As the two detectives headed back to the car, they heard Morgan check in over the radio.

"Kenny. I'm up to my knees in mud. I just came out of what looks like an abandoned shed in the marsh by the train station."

Becker raised his voice in an attempt to reach Madson as he stomped down the stairs of the home towards the car.

"This situation just got much more complicated."

"You can say that again." Madson retorted without turning his head.

"This situation..."

"Shut up and get in the car!"

Becker slid his hands into his pants pockets and smiled silently as he strolled behind his partner. Reports would come in from locations all around town; two from the State Park, two from the basements of Downtown bars, and more from older buildings on Broadway that had been banks or hotels. The entrance near the train station was unnerving because the train ran south to New York City and north towards Canada. Access to the railway in turn meant that the person or persons responsible for the death of Charles Cross could be anywhere by now.

XAVIER

Nathan's instincts were dead on; everyone in the VIP room of Club Decadence was indeed waiting for his reply to Xavier's question.

Was everything to his liking?

Honestly, he couldn't have been happier. It was as if someone knew his darkest desires and made them a reality. He couldn't complain about three super hot girls, elite VIP treatment, and free drinks. Yet a little voice in his head told him it was all very sudden, which it certainly was. It was all just a little too good to be true.

"Everything is fantastic. Thank you, Mr. Thrallson."

"Please call me Xavier. Your father would have wanted it that way." Xavier spread a toothy grin.

"I couldn't imagine anything nicer, Xavier."

"Really, I'm willing to wager you could," Xavier added and quickly replaced his grin.

Nathan was caught off guard by this last statement. He could sense that Xavier's grin was intended to comfort him but it felt like a mix between the Cheshire Cat and Jaws.

"What do you mean sir?"

"Sir. Why still so formal, Nathan? I simply mean that this way of life isn't out of your reach. Evenings such as this could be an everyday occasion for someone like you."

"Like me?" Nathan mused.

"Indeed, someone exactly like you."

Nathan was sure there was more to this than Xavier was telling him. Did Xavier feel obligated to him in some way because of his father's death? Time seemed to blur and move slowly as Nathan contemplated the meaning behind his host's words, all the while Xavier's toothy grin waited for a response. His ice-blue stare was mesmerizing and frightening at the same time. Nathan noticed that the guests around him seemed to be going about their business while also keeping an attentive ear on the conversation between Xavier and him.

"What do you mean by someone like me?"

"I mean that you are a significant link in a chain of events. A chain your father began."

Nathan responded a bit severely before his brain could filter his reply. The implication of his father's involvement seemed to sting him.

"How so?"

Xavier extended his giant cold and clammy hand to rest on the top of Nathan's own hand. He spoke as if to a child.

"Nathan please do not misunderstand me. I realize your father's death is still fresh upon you. I simply intend to illuminate you.

I want to reveal to you a part of your father's life you were not aware of. Your father was part of something big, something bigger than you and bigger than me. We are part of it, that much is true, but it is far more reaching than us. It reaches farther than this city or country. I'm talking about something that would change the world as we know it."

Xavier's words were compelling and eased Nathan's worries. Surely Xavier was referring to some benevolent yet lucrative endeavor his father had failed to mention.

"Well, you have my interest."

"Good," Xavier removed his hand from Nathan's and clasped them together as if making a prayer with his fingertips resting on his chin.

"Let's say I have a proposition for you, Nathan."

"I'm all ears." Nathan twisted in his seat to face his host.

Xavier twisted as well and leaned in close to Nathan. He clasped Nathan's hand between both of his. He looked Nathan dead in the eye.

"Nathan, I need you to pick up where your father left off."

ANTIQUUS LIBELLUS
SERVATOR JOHN THOMAS

Between the colonization of new territories and exploration efforts, it would seem the Gläm had secured a foothold in the Americas and Europe. An aspect that is often underestimated is that they do not only have control over their hosts but also over other people. It's hard to directly determine how they achieve the "sway" they hold over others; it may be due to pheromones, telepathic suggestion, or even skin contact. Whatever the means by which it is accomplished, the result is an amplified charisma. This effect on others becomes crucial during negotiations and other dealings. Needless to say, the trade and land agreements that transpired early on in the settling of North America provided ample opportunities for the Gläm to establish their presence.

The particulars of the geography of North America also helped. The existence of waterways that traveled from the sea inland provided easy access. The Hudson River allowed them to move from the Atlantic into and throughout the Northeast.

It was there at the foothills of the Adirondack Mountains that a branch of the Gläm settled. Initially, it was the Hudson that allowed them access but ultimately it was the vast network of springs and the underground channels they carved that provided them an outpost. The area was speckled with waterways and lakes which they liked very much but also over the years there was just the type of activity they thrived on; battles, land grabbing, gambling, and debauchery.

The Gläm had pioneers of their own. Some headed west toward the Great Lakes to further spread their influence and increase their numbers. Others ventured north in the Adirondacks where they eventually took advantage of droves of people looking to improve vitality and respiration, only to succumb to the Gläm's schemes. But the Gläm took a particular liking to Saratoga Springs; an abundance of springs and waterways throughout, the turning point of the Revolutionary War, and access to the Hudson, all of these were attractive but gamblers proved to be an easy mark for them. So they settled in and found that Saratoga Lake, surrounded by Lake Houses where money changed hands and booze flowed was to their liking. It all suited them just fine. It was at one of those Lake Houses, Riley's, that Mr. Augustus Cross set in motion the events that led to my own sister's death. I'm not certain which one of her boys will be reading this. When the Gläm starts going after them they'll come hard and fast. Unfortunately, both boys have weaknesses that the Gläm will try to exploit when recruiting them. Nathan in many ways has always been more like his father while Gavin has always been more like his mother. The scariest part is that they would settle for either one. All they need is a genetic match or connection. Either way, whichever one of Charlie's sons they get will be discarded in the end. Whatever little things that made them who they were will diminish over time while under the Gläms' control. One of the boys will be incorporated and the most devastating aspect is right up to the end, just before their bodies are tossed aside like husks, they'll believe that they'll be immortal, powerful, and wealthy. When all they have been is used.

71

THE DOCTOR'S CHALLENGE

The Doctor's proposition sent Gavin back to a time when he was about four or five at the zoo with Grandma. He felt caught, trapped. He remembered the exhibit that housed the Grizzlies. It was a manmade reconstruction of a rock cave. There was a little waterfall, a honeysuckle bush, and the ever-present cast iron fence that confined them in this space. Gavin could feel a huge whirling pit of despair and lost hope behind one bear's big complacent eyes. He could feel every rock tossed, every sneering, ugly face, every prod and poke. Most of all he felt sick, it felt as though something inside him wanted to burst out. His Grandma felt his grip tighten and looked down towards him and asked, "What's the matter, little one?"

He knew she was looking at him, but he couldn't pull his gaze away from the empty stare of the all-too-passive beast before him. As she scooped him up and headed for the next exhibit, he continued to stare at the thick, dark shadow and as it passed from his sight, he heard a bellow. He had never heard anything roar before but somehow he knew that this wasn't one. He was right. The sound was not pride but the lack thereof, he was listening to the anguish of a trapped wild thing.

That's how he felt sitting on Dr. Larson's sofa.

His Grandma took him in shortly after his mother died after the incident with his father. He was too young when she passed to really remember a lot about his mom. He did remember overhearing his Grandma talking to one of her old blue-haired friends. She could understand an accident at the mill taking her dear departed husband. She couldn't fathom why a rain-slicked road and a deer would take her only son's wife away. She looked over at him as he played in the dirt in the backyard. She was sitting at a picnic table where she and her friend were chatting. He heard her say in a distant yet loving tone.

"But, my Gavin, he and his brother Nathan are miracles. Both boys thrown from the same car their mother perished in. Both boys were tossed into a ravine filled with leaves, safe and sound, just a few scratches." She swung her hand in an upward motion at the sky and presumably at God as well. Gavin and Nathan's survival may have been a miracle, but their escape from that car was not.

He was suddenly returned from his thoughts to Dr. Larson's office. His flood of memories no doubt would be considered a moment contemplating the proposal. Dr. Larson said that these types of childhood memories could have been the root of his manic depression and his gripping agoraphobia. Dr. Larson said a lot of things about his childhood. He always talked about how Gavin's problems were all about what happened during his childhood, but not what his childhood was actually about in any detail. He seemed to want to avoid any actual event and focus on what he called the 'bigger picture.' He would speak in his nurturing but overbearingly condescending tone. He was a recovering hippy, a tall, thin man. He would flick his long stringy red hair over his shoulder as they spoke (probably to remember the portion missing from the top of his head). His fake snakeskin shoes, with a matching belt and waistline cell phone holder, matched perfectly with his style and cologne. He would tell him how he acknowledged and sympathized with the death and loss Gavin experienced as a child. He often mentioned how his mother's death was the cause of this and that.

The doctor used to put him under. He would listen to his voice and let his subconscious drift. The good doctor seemed bent on pounding it into Gavin's head that the horrific evening with his father never happened. He told him his love for nature was an escapist tactic; he was always telling Gavin that everything that was natural to him was unnatural. He made him feel that those things that he felt were the most basic and essential, made him a freak, in Gavin's terms. The doctor used words that were educated euphemisms. Gavin could sense that the doctor was growing tired of his stubborn grip on what he called his paranoid and often schizophrenic delusions. His animosity began to build up after the years of the same "thing" from Gavin.

Dr. Larson asked him, "Gav?" Larson's nose chased his eyebrows as they arched upwards, and his hand came to rest on his chin. "Gavin, what would you say if I thought that you have been living a delusion ever since that night with your father? And what you call human weakness and depravity: the city, technology, modern luxuries, the things not necessary for existence, as you put it, were actually quite beneficial? And that I felt you were weak and that if you were truly a man, as you say you wish to be, you would accept a challenge. You're a big boy now. Right? Huh, whaddya say?"

Gavin looked at the doctor, he spread his arms along the back of the sofa. He knew the doctor was trying to wind him up. He replied calmly, "How can I refuse an offer like that?" making an effort to sound as undaunted as possible. That always pissed the doctor off.

"Well," Larson began, "Why don't we play a little game of hide-and-go-seek my way?" He then stood up, walked out of his office door, and got into the mahogany elevator doors. Gavin jumped up, sprinted down the hall, and stood beside him in the elevator. His office was in downtown Albany. It would seem that the doctor wanted to push Gavin's limits. In actuality, he wanted to do him in now that Gavin had been cornered. The doors closed and they were gone.

Down on the street, Gavin tried to keep an eye on Larson. He had given him till the count of forty. Gavin may have had long legs strong enough to carry him more quickly than the doctor, but it was easy to lose someone on the street. Larson quickly passed people on the sidewalk. It wasn't quite lunch hour but the offices in the area must have been on a coffee break. The sidewalks were filled with people in blazers carrying briefcases. Larson began to weave in between the people attached to those briefcases. It was official that Gavin had lost him in the crowd. He looked around frantically. Larson was seated about forty yards up the street on a cast iron bench, his arms hung along its back. He sat there snickering, waiting for Gavin to find him. Larson's hand flew to his waist and grabbed his cellular phone. He had received another text.

-You are being followed by an unknown person. Do not proceed as planned. Some place more private.

-X

Gavin heard it and made a beeline for the now-preoccupied doctor and his phone. He walked up behind him and tapped him on the shoulder,

"Gotcha," he smiled.

Larson punched the power button on his phone, "So you have, but I have to go," he said as he stood up, looking Gavin in the eye. "See you next week."

Gavin had been visiting Dr. Larson for years. For years he heard nothing but terms such as agoraphobia, escapist, and other phrases that sting. Gavin was an escapist because he ran into the woods to "escape" the real world. He was agoraphobic because he preferred the country to the forest of cars, buildings, and people in the city. Dr. Larson tried to tell him that everything he thought was helping was wrong. His Grandma encouraged him to find ways to soothe his fears. She had always taken him for walks in the woods as a child. They would collect thimbleberries; watch birds and just mosey along. He

76

continued the practice as he grew older. He always found the serenity he was looking for in nature. That was until that terrible day when his Grandma passed on. She was a wonderful woman and deserved to die peacefully and with her dignity. She was a shining example of old age and good timing. She swore she would live to see him graduate. She did, and she also watched him turn eighteen as she closed her eyes for the last time. She was so proud of him.

After the funeral, Gavin was told that he inherited a small sum of money. He was also told that he was the owner of Grandma's home as well as a cabin up north and the surrounding hundred acres. Apparently, the place once belonged to his parents. It was a gift from some eccentric and wealthy relative, on his father's side. It was only used once for their honeymoon. He decided to spend some time up there after his odd morning with Dr. Larson. He thought that it would be the perfect place to deal with things. That notion was in so many ways contrary to the beliefs and practices of Dr. Larson. His Grandma was the only family he had ever had. It was a crushing blow to lose her, so close to graduating from high school, and on his birthday. He handled everything with poise and strength.

He headed to the cabin after leaving Albany. It was a straight shot on 87 North to North Creek. To his surprise, the place had been cleaned and stocked up. It was in disrepair when he first visited some time ago. Hard work was never an obstacle for him. Since the place was settled it would afford him a lot of time to think.

That afternoon, while investigating the bedroom, on a tiny shelf near the bed, he perused a small collection of books. He figured that they were most likely a gift from that eccentric nameless relative since his parents had only spent one night there. There were five small books in all. The first was a training manual of sorts for meditation; it covered a spectrum of diverse cultural techniques. The next two were Celtic and Native American folklore. A collection of transcendental poetry and a small leather-bound journal. He skimmed them one by one. It helped to keep his mind off things.

The journal was the last book he read. He was anxious to read it after wondering about the cryptic notes he found in the margins of the other books. The journal started off with a rambling account of the life of its owner. He seemed to be a person who shared many of the same views as Gavin, although he couldn't exactly parallel the experiences with ones of his own, the things he spoke of were all way too similar. Whomever the journal belonged to had experienced many a devastating loss in life and retreated here. The unknown writer spoke of how: "The only way in which to disengage completely from society is distance. The only way to be free from society is submission to Nature. Man forgot, in his arrogance, that his dominance had a cost. The Tao of Nature was forgotten." The journal went on to give detailed mediations, and mantras as well as directions to a favored spot for meditation. Gavin couldn't stop reading. He forced himself to flip to the inside cover with a name scrawled in cursive.

John Thomas

John Thomas. That was his uncle, his mom's brother. They

had never met but he had heard that he fell off the face of the Earth after his sister died. Gavin was beyond curious now.

He flipped back to the portion containing the directions. They lead to a trail not too far from the cabin. The trail wound through the forest to a point where two rings of moss-covered rocks sat one within the other for what appeared to be centuries.

Sitting down in the middle, he lay back and thought of the meditation. He wasn't sure when he passed from consciousness, but waking up he found himself, astonishingly revitalized.

Possessed with newly found energy, he ran back to the cabin and picked up the journal once again. He reread the stories in the books with notes in the margins. These notes were referred to in the journal. Some of the marginalia dealt with Jack O' the Green. The fairy tale was about a man who is one with nature and is its protector. Some of the comments revolved around the myth of the Wendigo; a person in Native American legend, with such a strong affinity for nature that they must leave everything behind. The person would give themselves to nature. Their only desire was her blessing and her gifts. There were also conflicting stories regarding the Wendigo from the Northwest where the Wendigo was seen as a cannibal figure. There were copious notes in the journal that referred to texts that were missing from the shelf and a man named Bobby who sounded like an instructor of sorts. He was intrigued.

Gavin decided to go to the same place over the next few days and meditate, hoping each day another layer would unfurl. The concepts seemed interwoven. They were pieced together in a sort of manual, or practice. He thought he was beginning to follow them. He had never taken to anything like this. The entries made sense to him. Soon, they began to talk about his family.

The entries regarding his family had his head spinning so he opted to go to bed early. In his dreams, he saw Dr. Larson in his fancy sports car. He was pulled up outside the cabin, honking and hollering that he had found him and that he couldn't escape this time. The full moon created a glare on the windshield. The smell of exhaust and cheap cologne was bitter in his nose. He felt his stringy hair in his hand as he wrapped his hand around his ponytail from behind. He turned, and when he saw him, he was silent. His face was frozen. The same expression was on it as he lay, lifeless, on the hood. There was a ring of broken glass on the smashed hood. He heard his damn phone ringing and knew this was real. Frantic, he looked around. He was short of breath and disoriented. The moon was full and high overhead. The red hairs fell from his grip as he saw headlights approaching. He began to run. "Gavin!" someone hollered.

"Gavin, it's okay. It's your Uncle John."

The pickup rolled slowly forward and came to a gravel-crunching stop. Gavin was so out of it that he couldn't make anything out beyond the glare of the headlights. The door swung open and a voice came from the figure approaching.

"Gavin, I've been following the doctor. Otherwise, I'd have been here when you got here."

Gavin's heart was about to burst. He crouched down holding onto the side of Larson's Porsche hoping not to puke. "What's going on?"

"The doctor was going to kill you."

"What?"

"Carefully reach in his coat pocket. There is a needle intended for you in there."

Gavin's legs nearly went out from under him as he tried to stand. His hand was trembling as he reached into the pocket. He pulled out a syringe.

"He would have killed you."

"Why?"

Uncle John came over to Gavin, he was big and tall, and he rested his hand on his shoulder. Gavin could feel John's hand begin to tremble as he spoke.

"Because you were in the way. Just like your mother."

A gurgling chirping noise was coming from the doctor's body. The two men crept slowly toward its head. John pulled a mini flashlight from his pocket and shone it on the doctor's face. His dead eyes were still but his mouth appeared to be moving. His lower jaw opened. A shiny black head appeared in the light. A thing about a foot long slumped forward onto the red dented hood of the sports car. Its skin was like a salamander's its head a cross between a snake and a tadpole. It had no arms or legs; barbs or spikes ran along the length of its spine.

"And there's the cause of all our family's misery. If he was coming for you, Nathan is in real trouble. I have a lot to fill you in on."

Gavin stood there speechless, his fingertips digging into the hood of the car, his mouth gaping, eyes unblinking. He had no idea what the hell was going on here. He did realize one thing at that moment. What he saw as a kid was real. There was no denying it.

ANTIQUUS LIBELLUS

SERVATOR JOHN THOMAS

Upon hearing of Charles' death, the sense of urgency became palpable. The Gläm would make a move on the boys. They no doubt have been monitored for years. People have been placed in their lives or in their paths for some time now. Any events or actions that may have precluded them from serving as hosts have been scrutinized by the Gläm intensely. Either one of them would be the final host for an "Immortal," a third stage Gläm. Gavin and Nathan have been guarded over by them. The crash that took Maggie's life somehow left them unharmed. I have no doubt now that they were responsible both for her death and the boys' salvation. As glad as I am that they survived they lost their mother because she was inconvenient. She was an obstacle to the Gläms' endgame so she needed to be removed. So, they were robbed of their mother and forced to live without her.

Charles must have known what was in store for his sons. Part of me wants to believe he didn't have a hand in Maggie's death. By now he is no longer the Charles he was. So, he may not truly care for the fate of his boys. He has been

Thrall

so interwoven with the Gläm that any shred of him prior to being a host is nothing more than a mask to keep appearances. His instincts and experiences are at their disposal. The Gläm exists in a perpetual state of retribution punishing humanity for being in the way. The goal has always been to make the planet more habitable for them. As their numbers increase ours will dwindle. Humanity will exist as long as we are useful. Once they have leeched off of us enough to breathe the air and walk on land without us our role as a food source will be exhausted. No doubt they will behave as we have as the dominant species. When the planet is dark enough, damp enough, and warm enough the Gläms' ShangriLa will be complete and our species will be a memory.

UNCLE JOHN'S RESEARCH

John pulled a pair of leather working gloves from one back pocket and a gallon-size freezer bag from the other. Gavin watched his motions, still in a state of shock from what he had witnessed. John pulled the gloves on over his big, calloused hands. From Gavin's viewpoint, his knuckles looked like they were the size of golf balls. Gavin was no stranger to hard work either but he knew his uncle was as tough and determined as he looked. Without any hesitation, John grabbed hold of the spiny thing on the hood. He held it as if it were a puppy or a kitten in its mother's maw. It was limp and lifeless and suspended from the scruff of its neck.

Uncle John dumped it in the bag and sealed it. He tossed it unceremoniously in the direction of his driver's side door. John walked around and popped the latch to open the Porsche's trunk. He then similarly manhandled the corpse of Dr. Larson and shoved it in. He threw the car in neutral and steered it while pushing from the driver's side door behind the cabin. He then collected the creature in the bag and drove his pickup in behind the Porsche. John turned off the truck and collected both his nephew and his specimen, then took Gavin indoors and sat him down at a table by the fireplace.

John lit a candle on the table with a match from a big box from the kitchen. He put the candle down on the table and proceeded to start a pot of coffee.

John then went into the bedroom and returned with another journal. He tossed it spinning sideways into the center of the table beside the candle. The flame bent and flickered before regaining its shape. The word "Servator" had been burned into the cover of the leather journal. John placed both hands on the table and leaned across to speak to Gavin.

"Gavin, I know you are freaked out right now. I need you to hear it. All of it. And we don't have much time before they get here."

"Who gets here?" Gavin asked, truly lost.

"Larson's buddies!"

"Oh," Gavin thought he grasped things, "the text messages Larson was getting."

"Cell phones!" John slammed his hand down on the table. "These damn things don't need cell phones. They are all part of the same thing!"

Gavin let out an exasperated sigh and leaned back in his chair. "All right I'm lost again."

John plopped down in the chair and slid his hand down over

his face. He looked across the table at Gavin and cocked his head to one side. The coffee began to percolate on the stove. He motioned to Gavin to get the coffee and some cups. Gavin obeyed dutifully and sat down with two cups of black coffee.

"Gavin, we are going to drink that pot of coffee. I'm going to tell you everything I know and then we are going to drive Larson's car to the quarry and set it on fire. Then we are going to try and save your brother."

"Sounds like a plan. Deranged, but a plan." Gavin's sarcasm wasn't lost on John. He simply ignored it.

"Do you know how they say all life sprang forth from the sea?"

"Yup, I know evolution and all that."

"Well, these things came from the sea. They started at the very bottom, a very long time ago. You know what a Hydra is? It is a little tentacled thingy that if you chop off a piece it turns into a whole new one."

Gavin nodded in agreement.

"So, imagine a little seaward like that. Every time you slice and dice it, it turns into a couple more of them. Now mix in a whole new factor. These things are like DNA parasites. They eat flesh and are able to absorb any living thing's programming. I've paid scientists to run tests on these things, all under the table, and they were baffled by the number of different creatures that were intertwined in these things. So, they feed on whatever swims around the bottom of the sea for years taking whatever attributes from those creatures they find useful: Coelacanths, Hagfish, Remoras, Sharks, Anglerfish, Eels, you name it. They evolve and change based on whatever they eat. They learn to swim, produce armor, and even how to control other creatures from the inside. These things have used water as a means of travel since they came about. Then they start hitching rides in all manner of creatures. Eventually, they get a hold of bigger and bigger creatures, dinosaurs, and eventually us.

"Think about how many cultures have vanished after years of prosperity. Tenochtitlan, the Aztec city that was built on a lake. The Romans had aqueducts piping water everywhere. The more humans they fed on the smarter they got. Most of the stories I have got are from people like us. People who decided to get to the bottom of things when their loved ones turned up dead. These things have been in North America since the Vikings. I heard a story from an Abenaki guy who lost his brother to them. He told me that he got a story from one of the elders that involved what he thought were the earliest stories about them. A Viking group landed on shore and they had a frozen corpse with them. As far as they could make out it was adrift at sea. They told the people that after they traded with them they would burn his body in a boat and shove it out to sea. The people helped the Vikings in their preparations set the body ablaze and shoved the boat floating into the water. They gathered in solemn reverence and observation. The groups of people were amazed when they saw something stirring in the water moving towards them. The body came on shore in a rush and savagely seized one of the Viking men. The smoldering corpse pinned him to the ground and vomited something into his mouth. The reanimated body fell still on the man. He screamed and thrashed for a moment and then appeared fine. I was told that that Viking's name was Glämson. Since then, they have been called Gläm.

"So, say these things are real," Gavin interrupted hesitantly. "How do they get around on land?"

"That's why they need us. It's all there in the journal. I've got as much information on these things as anybody else does. They have these spikes, see."

John slid the bag towards Gavin.

"They slither down your throat, jab their spikes into your spine and they're jacked into your system."

Gavin felt his hands sliding up and down on his knees. It was an unconscious motion. He wasn't cold or shivering. It was as if his body knew he should have been shivering but his brain was too busy.

"How does my family figure into all this?" Gavin's gaze was on his now still hands.

CROSSROADS

Nathan wasn't sure what was going on. Xavier was right in his face asking him to pick up where his father left off. He didn't know what that even meant and once again he had the pressing feeling that everyone was waiting to hear his response.

Xavier's gaze was direct and cold. Nathan felt that his host's unblinking stare was somehow aware of his uncertainty, weighing and analyzing his thoughts. As uncomfortable as Nathan found this line of questioning, what struck him as odd was that for whatever reason he couldn't look away.

"What exactly does that mean?" Nathan knew how apprehensive he sounded.

Xavier slid his hands away from Nathan's. They recoiled like a serpent in retreat and found a resting place on his lap. Xavier slumped in his throne-like chair as if exhausted and disinterested. He sighed quietly. "Nathan, it is really very simple. I by no means intended to be cryptic. Your father and I met a long time ago. He was a young man then." Xavier's demeanor became more reassuring as he began to explain. He seemed pleased to be in control of the flow of conversation once again. "Your father was quite young when we met. I was an associate of your Grandfather, Augustus. Gus was what he went by. You may remember him. Or had he already passed when you were born?"

Nathan was puzzled. He screwed up his face as if he was thinking hard but he really hadn't had any idea who his Grandfather was. "I think he died when I was too young to remember," Nathan offered.

"Yes, I think you're right. Gus has been gone a long time now and now your father as well." Xavier's hand hovered for a moment and settled on Nathan's knee in an awkward gesture of condolence. Nathan regarded the hand in a quizzical fashion as if a strange insect had perched on his knee. He felt that his gaze was lingering and had to make an effort to look up and away from Xavier's hand.

"Your Grandfather, he used to love to play cards. He actually was a regular at many of the gambling houses that were on Saratoga Lake many years ago. We met at Riley's Lakehouse during its heyday. He was quite the cool customer at the tables. Yet he had a habit of trying to make up for his losses at the table instead of knowing when to say when. It was this tendency of his that had initially gotten us acquainted."

Xavier paused for a moment of reflection resting his chin on his hand and staring off into the distance.

"He was a proud man," Xavier began again. "He would

rather burn than take a handout. A man like him wasn't one to ask for help. You may remember that he and your Grandmother weren't swimming in money. They got by on what they had from his work at the paper mill. Well, Gus got himself into a little hot water with a rough customer who had lent him some money. When he couldn't cough up the money this thug threatened Gus' family. That was the point in time where I became involved."

Xavier straightened himself as if to reassure Nathan that he was a man of some consequence, an important man who was a force to be reckoned with.

"It was a small matter to cover Gus' loan and arrange different terms. Gus was so taken by my intervention in this matter that he nearly shook my hand off in thanks. A strong man indeed, he was wrought of iron after so many years at the mill. He assured me that he would repay me the sum he owed me just as soon as he could pull some overtime without the missus taking notice. I assured him the money was of no import. It was not my motivation in the matter."

Xavier paused. He exhaled heavily and his hands went once again into a prayer-like steeple, index fingers resting on his lips. His eyes were guarding some secret and Nathan noticed the mystery in his aspect.

"Did he ever get you the money?" Nathan asked in a youthful, almost hurt way, as if his nearly unknown Grandfather was still in arrears on the loan.

Xavier lowered his hands and turned to face Nathan. His expression was earnest but exaggerated as if to make his response heartfelt. "He repaid me in full, although there was no money involved in our arrangement. You see, Nathan, I invest in people. I offer help to those in need. When someone is at a desperate crossroads in life, I step in. Often this investment is simply on an individual basis but in special cases, as was your Grandfather's, it is an entire family."

"So, you knew my grandmother as well?"

"No. I never had the pleasure of her company. You see Nathan, some things are between men. My work is man's work and often women don't seem to comprehend or appreciate what I do."

"Oh, I see." Nathan didn't see. He still had no idea what it was Xavier actually provided for his family.

"So, as per our arrangement, Gus introduced me to your father, and as they say that is how the story begins."

ROADTRIP

Gavin followed his uncle's truck in Larson's mid-life crisis car. He would normally have jumped at the chance to drive a sports car like Larson's, but under the circumstances, the ten-minute drive down Route Nine to the quarry seemed like it took an hour. It was dark and he nearly drove off the cliff of the quarry into the dark waters below. His uncle had swung his truck sideways near the edge, his red taillights leaving a serpent tail of red light his wheels throwing up dust, and Gavin had thought that he had another thirty feet to spare. His uncle hollered, snapping him out of his white-knuckled daze.

"Whoa!"

Uncle John hollered as he jumped in front of the car, both hands extended forward as if to physically stop the car himself, from the look of his forearms he very well may have been able to. Gavin jammed on the brakes and yanked the wheel to the left, gravel crunching and flying through the night and clanking against the side of his uncle's truck.

"Simmer down, Gav!"

Gavin exhaled heavily and slumped his head forward as though reaching his destination had allowed some form of torment to cease. He had been driving with a dead body in the trunk, so his tension was responded to with compassion by his uncle.

"We can't leave the good doctor in the trunk," Uncle John spoke in a kind but teasing tone. "It won't look like much of an accident with him locked in the trunk."

Uncle John moved to the back of the vehicle. He yelled for Gavin to pop the trunk. Gavin's hands were still gripping the wheel like a vice. He heard his uncle but couldn't reply. His mind told his body to move, to respond but nothing happened. His uncle reached down the side of the driver's seat and popped the latch himself. He then opened the door and gave Gavin an upward tug under the arm. Gavin slowly became aware of standing up and the daze he was in seemed to slowly dissipate like mist.

"Come on there, big fella'. Let's get this over with." John led Gavin around to the trunk. Facing them curled into a fetal position, was the body of Dr. Larson. His dead eyes stared back at them. His mouth was gaping in an exaggerated silent scream, and dark runnels of blood slithered from the corners of his lower lip. They hoisted him out and propped him behind the wheel. John told Gavin to leave the car running. Gavin watched as he walked to his truck and came back with the biggest sledgehammer he had ever seen.

"That a twenty-pounder?" Gavin asked.

"Yup, I've had this beauty for years."

95

John smashed the driver's side light out. Then the hood got a couple whacks and the fender above the wheel. He then proceeded to smash a large piece of rubble near the edge of the cliff. He must have felt Gavin's questioning glance.

"So, they think he crashed!"

"Oh…good thinking."

They rolled the car backward and lined it up. John motioned for Gavin to step back, then took out his knife and slit the sleeve of the doctor's shirt and ripped off a long piece. He removed the gas cap stuffed the piece down in and secured the cap again. He motioned to Gavin to throw the car into drive. Gavin did and the vehicle slowly rolled forward. John lit the shirt sleeve on fire as the vehicle neared the edge. The vehicle fell a lot more quietly than Gavin expected, at least until it exploded as they were driving away, the truck actually rocked a bit from the explosion.

"Now we save Nathan's ass."

Gavin nodded silently.

"It's four hours to Manhattan. I hope we make it in time."

ANTIQUUS LIBELLUS

SERVATOR JOHN THOMAS

I've been trying to keep tabs on Nathan down in the city. He took work at his father's firm and no doubt has been surrounded by Gläm hosts. My assumption is that he will be the most heavily recruited of the two boys. A couple of reasons are; he is the most like his father, he works in and amongst them all day, and Immortals are based in New York City.

Gavin is a different case. Although he would work as an heir and host, he poses somewhat of a problem for the Gläm. He is more like his mother. He is erratic because he is driven more by emotion than ambition. This quality has caused trouble for him most of his life and would be an uncontrolled element in the eyes of those who are pursuing him. They are pursuing him. I've been able to track Gavin's movements and have seen them watching him. He's oblivious, of course. With all that's been going on for him he's been even more distracted than usual.

The concern I have is that both boys will be taken. Nathan as an heir and host would be lost but Gavin may be eliminated simply because he poses a

Thrall

threat like his mother did.

My hope is that if I can get Gavin's head out of the clouds, he may be able to help me save both of them.

CONNECTIONS

Madson and Becker were silent on the drive to the train station. It was only a few minutes away and there was hardly any traffic. The radio chatter seemed to be mostly about the can of worms they had opened and the nature of the talk on the airways was full of childlike curiosity. The two detectives were far less than playful; there was no hint of glee in the business at hand. It was quietly evident to both of them that before this was resolved it was going to get worse. They couldn't have been more accurate even if they didn't give breath to the thoughts coursing through their heads. It was going to get worse.

The train station sits just off of West Ave, back behind a long straight stretch guarded by pines. Madson and Becker pulled up along the cement curve and parked right on the side of the cul-de-sac. They were met by the officer who had discovered the exit from the tunnels to the train station.

"Detectives," the officer, Morgan was his name, greeted them with a nod, yet his head remained looking at the ground.

Madson and Becker knew the routine.

"What is it?" Madson asked directly.

"Well, sir… I don't really know how to say… but it's like nothing I've ever seen." Morgan looked younger somehow, his gaze still on the ground like he was about to be grounded for sassing his folks.

"Come on, out with it!" The impatience in Becker's tone surprised Madson and Morgan. This whole escapade was getting to him which worried Madson as Becker was usually the cool and collected type.

"Bodies sir, piles of them. We found a tunnel heading away from here underneath Church St. towards the hospital. It was between the hospital and the golf course. I called for the coroner just as soon as I saw them. But they weren't right."

"They're dead, of course, they're not right!" Madson interjected trying to add some levity to the grim happenings. Becker was still and staring out across the train tracks.

"I know," Morgan finally looked up but avoided their eyes his gaze was up and beyond their heads like he was looking off in the direction of the hospital. He began to speak, the lump in his throat moving, working hard. He was somewhere between tears and vomiting. He wrung his hands.

"They were all naked, but they…" His hand went up to his mouth to stifle emotion or perhaps nausea. "They were all skinned, except for their heads. There were piles of them heaped on top of each other, rotten ones on the bottom, swollen ones on top. The smell was…"

Morgan threw up on his muddy feet. He tottered backward and Madson swung wide of the mess on the ground and grabbed his shoulder.

"It's alright man." Madson clapped him on the back and looked over at Becker with a wry grin. Becker didn't return the glance; his gaze was off in the distance. Behind his eyes, the pieces of this puzzle were not falling in place and he could just not figure out how all of this connected.

DECISIONS

Nathan was still stuck on what exactly Xavier had done for his family. He understood how he became involved with the family but to what extent still mystified him. His confusion must have been apparent because precisely at that moment, as if he had read his mind, Xavier began to speak again.

"As I have said, I invest in people. I can tell you are struggling with what that means. What I have to tell you may seem improbable, but I urge you to suspend your disbelief until I have clarified things for you." Xavier pushed himself back into his chair sitting up straight as if to address the masses.

"You need to understand that I knew your father and Grandfather very well. You could say I knew what made them tick. At times I knew them better than they knew themselves, I could comprehend their true nature. I appreciated them for that very reason. Deep down we were very much alike. We wanted power. Isn't that what all men truly desire? For some that equals wealth, others political position, physical prowess, and for some, even the allure of fame and adoration." Xavier's eyes surveyed the room and he knew before he looked, that everyone in attendance was listening to him.

For some reason, Xavier's words stung Nathan. He spoke vehemently with more intensity than he would have wished.

"Power? My dad?"

Xavier seemed to be expecting this sort of response.

"Power, as I've said, has many different forms. Your family had a hunger for power in its purest and most unadulterated form: knowledge. Surely, you've heard the old saying, 'Knowledge is power.' Gus' preoccupation with cards and your father's success with the stock market are not singular. They both wanted to be aware of things before they happened. They didn't seek the power of prophecy. They sought the ability to read the behavior and faces of their fellow man as well as how to interpret situations in ways that would lead to personal success. I would fathom you could relate to such inklings. Have you not a bit of them in you? Don't you sometimes find yourself longing at times to know what others do not?"

Once again Xavier had read Nathan's thoughts, he had encapsulated an entire interior dialogue in a few words. It was becoming unsettling that Nathan's words had begun to be snatched from his mind before they reached his lips. In response, he felt himself nod like a dumbfounded child caught red-handed in some sneaky endeavor.

"So, you do? I was confident you had potential. Gavin never struck me as the type."

"Gavin? How do you know Gav?" Nathan had spoken

103

impulsively again. His words surged out when Xavier brought up his family disparagingly.

"I have an idea about who he is. We have never met. But you and I had never met until this evening, yet I have an idea of who you are Nathan. Why else would I have sought you out over Gavin?

"Have you been spying on us?" Nathan's tone was getting severe.

"No such thing. Spying is such a derogatory concept. Due to my investment in your family, it was necessary to protect that investment. I would feel more comfortable with a more benevolent phrase; 'keeping tabs' perhaps. I assure you my motivation for doing so was entirely in your best interest."

"So why did you bring me here tonight?"

"As I have said, I need you to pick up where your father left off. You need to think of this as an amazing opportunity. Imagine the success experienced by your father and Grandfather."

"My father was successful. My Grandfather lived a very modest life though." Nathan's tone belied that he was searching for answers and Xavier was ready to provide them.

"Indeed. Gus did provide for his family in a modest fashion but I assure you that with our assistance he was quite a success. He amassed a small fortune with his card playing. A great portion of those funds were secreted away by yours truly. As a provision of our arrangement, I insisted that he do so for your father."

"Is that where Dad got the money to invest?"

"Yes. When the time was right, I approached him as I had

done with you. I pointed him in the right direction and he was quite pleased with the outcome. Your father has put aside funds for you just as your Grandfather did for him. Now, there is a question which remains unanswered."

Nathan's eyes grew wide. His curiosity peeked. Xavier looked him in the eye and asked, "Are you interested?"

THE RUNDOWN

Uncle John could see the Tappan Zee Bridge in the distance. He reached over and shook Gavin's shoulder to wake him.

"Gav, wake up."

"Huh, I'm awake." Gavin wiped the drool from the corner of his mouth with his sleeve. His neck was stiff. A truck window doesn't make the best of pillows.

"Listen," Uncle John began as he dug for his wallet. "You need to know about what and who we are dealing with here. Most of it is written down in the journal I gave you, in case anything should happen." John's gaze was locked on traffic. Gavin didn't like the sound of what he was implying.

"What do you mean if anything happens?"

"If I end up dead." John's tone was irritated with a hint of condescension. "What the hell did you think I meant?"

"I was afraid that's what you meant." Gavin didn't want to say it out loud, but he couldn't imagine his reunion with Uncle John being cut short so quickly.

"Here's the rundown. These things are wired. They have like a cell phone built into them. They all know what happened to Dr. Larson. What they don't know is that instead of running from them we're coming at them. We need to get to Nathan before he's taken in by them."

"I still don't know what they want from Nathan and me."

"They need one of you to complete the Legacy."

"Legacy?"

"Okay, this is how it works. These things need us to live. They need to slowly steal our humanity, and DNA, so they can be human. From what I understand, what's been told to me, and from what I've found out is that these things work slowly. Think about it. They've always been around leeching from creatures till they reached the top of the food chain. They can be linked to the fall of tons of different cultures. But what is at the heart of their connection to civilizations that ended catastrophically is twofold. One aspect is water, the other is a rise to power. Dinosaurs came from the sea. Rome had aqueducts. Tenochtitlan was on a lake. Roanoke was near the coast. New York City, well you get it."

John became quiet, both of his hands gripping the wheel.

"Why us?" Gavin asked hesitantly.

"Well, one of you is next. Like I said, they are patient. They can wait. It takes three generations to pop one out that is able to get along on its own. Larson was only in the first stage. They got Gus, your dad, and now they need you or Nathan. I would bet that they counted on Nathan signing on and were just going to rub you out."

John's return to silence solidified the gravity of the situation in Gavin's mind.

"So, what happens if they get Nate?"

"It'll be the last step in the cycle. It takes like twenty years per person from what I figured out. In the end, they'll have a walking talking thing that can live for a real long time like a tortoise. It will be like a combination of your Grandpa, Dad, and Nathan. It will look like them, know everything they knew, and be linked to all the other things like them around the globe."

"I can't believe Grandpa Gus and Dad were involved in all this. I didn't really know Grandpa, but from what I remember he was a hell of a guy."

"That's the thing. You never really know. They're all just like normal. Maybe some quirky behavior or they go missing every now and again. Usually, it's the wives who know something is up. Their husbands cheat, become estranged, or want a divorce. On rare occasions, some wives try to interfere. So, they eliminate them like your Mom." John sighed and hung his head for a moment. "I'm sure your Grandma knew too. They never use women as hosts, only as food."

"Food?"

"They usually start off with a mistress. Once they are fed on it's all done. These things have something in their saliva. It's like morphine or heroin. The Gläm get people hooked and then feed on them till they're dead. Sometimes they use guys but usually their Peelers are women."

"Peelers, what do you mean?" Gavin's revulsion was evident. His mind swam with repressed memories of his own father's actions years ago.

"I call them Peelers. They are so high they don't seem to mind having their skin nibbled off. These things are on like the ultimate Atkin's diet, all meat all the time, and all kinds to boot. Think about how every culture has some myth about some creature munching on people; Vampires, Incubus, Wendigo"

Gavin felt like he was going to vomit.

"That's why we're headed to the Meat Packing District. They operate a couple of clubs there. Yet their hunger is a constant drawback, they're vulnerable when they feed. They have to expose themselves and are too distracted to communicate with their brothers. The Meat Packing District makes for a convenient location and cover. I'm thinking that they have Nathan there."

ANTIQUUS LIBELLUS

SERVATOR JOHN THOMAS

I've been watching Gavin. My people in NYC can't set foot in Nathan's building let alone get close to him while he's at work. It seems the Gläm knows who does and who doesn't belong at Pendulum Accounting. My assumption is that Nathan is too far in to get out. I'm certain at this point that Gavin's therapist is involved. I've followed Gavin only to discover that his therapist has been following him as well.

What is even scarier than his therapist plotting against him is that he has been doing it since he was a kid. Gavin started seeing him after the "incident" with his father, Charles. Gav caught his dad feeding and called the cops. And in true Charles' style, he spun it around to make it look like his own son had gone loco. I'm not one to make excuses for people but all this mess set Gavin on the path to ruin long ago. I can't help but feel for the guy. I'm hesitant to pull him in. He's emotional and at times it makes him irrational. But although my head says hold back, my gut says he's alright. My heart goes out to him but in situations involving the Gläm being alert and cautious is often best.

In the days that are coming things will happen fast. The unfortunate reality is that the outcome of what will happen with the two boys will have far-reaching repercussions. I can only surmise that after the Gläm has used up Nathan, the resulting Immortal that is created will have a purpose. That purpose most assuredly will be expanding into and controlling new territory. It may be necessary to kill him before that becomes a certainty.

PEELERS

Becker was lost in a sea of possibilities. He had never imagined he would be involved in a case like this. Most cops go their whole life on the job never having to deal with anything like this. The scene was already swarming with forensic guys, cops, and the coroner. There were already complications in that the coroner, who was second on the scene, said that from the rate of decomposition, the bodies at the bottom of the pile had been there for a really long time, long enough to be of historical importance. It complicated matters that were already complicated. Becker couldn't help but feel that someone had to know about this. That many bodies don't get dumped for such a long period of time without someone knowing about it. Madson was leaning against the car and consoling Morgan. Becker approached them slowly deep in contemplation.

"Let's head back to the Cross' house." His words found Madson, who in turn grasped Morgan's shoulder in a sympathetic gesture that also sent the message to move along. They moved to the car doors as Morgan wobbled to a bench to sit. They didn't speak for a while as they headed towards North Broadway. They sat waiting at a stoplight at the intersection of Church St. and Broadway. The directional signal was the only sound in the car, Madson hazarded to speak.

"Nobody smelled them. All those years and nobody could smell them."

"They're down pretty deep. If anyone caught a whiff, they probably thought it was sulfur water from the springs." Becker looked down at the dash seeing what was there in a hazy and distorted semblance.

"Someone knew." His words felt heavy but somehow Madson felt lighter after uttering them.

"You're precisely right," Becker replied.

Madson was starting to understand why Becker needed to get back to the Cross house.

"I think Charles Cross knew. He's dead, but there's got to be somebody else."

"His kids?" Madson was fishing with that one and he knew it.

"I don't know about the kids' involvement. But there is a connection between Cross ending up dead and those bodies under the hospital. I keep thinking that whoever has been depositing those bodies knows how Cross died, or more importantly why he died."

"The problem is we have no leads from either end of the situation. We've got nothing about Cross and the only thing we got on the dumped bodies is that the tunnel leads to his house." Madson turned left onto North Broadway.

"There's one other piece." Becker paused as if to add emphasis to his statement. "Those bodies have been accumulating for a long time."

"So, what does that give us?" Madson slowed to a stop in front of the Cross house. Yellow police tape swayed in the breeze diagonally preventing access to the front porch.

"It gives us that someone, more than likely some small group of people, has kept secret their assistance over a long period of time. I don't feel like Cross would have been lugging corpses down there. If I wanted to keep something like that from people, I would have a hard time putting out a help-wanted ad. It had to have been a family affair. Cross used this house as a summer home. So, who looked after it while he was gone?"

"Sometimes I think you are a friggin' genius!" Madson got out of the car and moved towards the house. Becker followed continuing the epiphany.

"Well, we don't know who it is yet. But there must be records of some kind."

Madson tore through the police tape. He reached for the door handle.

"Friggin' genius!"

LEGACY

"I am definitely interested."

Nathan hated how desperate his words sounded. He was suddenly overwhelmed with feelings of excitement and anticipation. He wondered if the time was right for him. Had Xavier sought him out for that reason? His mind swam with visions of himself living out a much loftier existence.

Beside him, Xavier's smile became warm and smug. He nodded in silent approval.

"Good! Now, as they say, membership has its benefits. As far as the business side of our endeavor is concerned, I have arranged for you to be an investor in a very promising hedge fund."

"That's marvelous. Thank you so very much. I really don't know what to say."

"You are quite welcome. Yet there is still the matter of the continuation of your father's affairs."

"Oh, I had assumed that the matter was addressed with the

investment." Nathan felt as though some integral piece of all this had eluded him.

"Nathan, at the risk of sounding cliché, nothing in life is free. I need you to pick up where your father left off. Surely you didn't think that my assistance was purely altruistic. Your Grandfather got things started and your father continued them. It is up to you to finish things. In exchange for your success, you must make a commitment to be a host for us. You will have financial freedom; you will never have to worry about money again. You will be connected to a network of the most powerful and rich men in the world. I can assure you that you will also find that you will be surprised at the abilities that will be at your disposal."

"What do you mean by host?"

"We need you to provide refuge for one of our brothers. You will provide shelter and accommodations for the same person your family did."

"How is that possible? Was this person a child when underneath my Grandfather's care?"

"Indeed. You might say that your Grandfather was a host during infancy. But let me be clear that this is no ordinary individual you will be entrusted to care for. You will be responsible for the protection and deliverance of an entity that will be like a god amongst men. More so a demigod, part divine and part human, you must also understand that your participation as a host will require a degree of personal sacrifice. Yet, as I have said, your involvement will help to usher in a truly incredible individual. Myself and my brothers will be eternally grateful to you. Of course, we will ensure that you are well provided for. Yet from this point, I must make it evident that you will be a host for the next twenty years and then, unfortunately, you will be no more."

"What? Are you saying I will be dead?" Nathan's delusions of grandeur came to a crashing stop.

"More like reborn." Xavier pivoted in his seat and leaned in closer to Nathan.

"What are we talking about here? I'm lost."

"You will host within your person," Xavier touched Nathan's chest with his index finger. "In here, inside of you a being that was hosted by your father and grandfather. I am not speaking metaphysically, it is a corporeal being that contains the sum of your family's thoughts and ideas as well as all of my brothers' consciousness since the dawn of time. When you are reborn, twenty years from now, you too will be included in this being and the world will bend to your will. The being that emerges will want for nothing and be able to bend mortals' wills. You will be included in a brotherhood that spans the globe and holds dominion covertly over most of the planet."

Nathan's jaw went uncontrollably slack. Normally if someone had uttered these sentiments, he would have instantly assumed they were nuts. Deep down he didn't doubt a single word Xavier had uttered. There wasn't even an iota of uncertainty. He simply looked into Xavier's gaze absolutely overwhelmed. In response to this, Xavier simply smiled and patted Nathan's knee with his hand. He stood up and Nathan did as well. He stretched an arm around Nathan's shoulders

Thrall

and began leading him to a room away from everyone else. He spoke as they moved slowly in unison.

"Nathan, in the end you will be just like me."

PURSUIT

Uncle John had grown quiet as they got into the city. He had the appearance of someone concentrating on driving but traffic was obviously not the only thing on his mind. Gavin felt as though the silence would smother him, so he interjected with the inevitable question.

"So, what's the plan?"

"I don't really have anything elaborate." John's tone was flat, almost distant. "I have an idea where they'll have him. It really is a matter of whether or not we get to him in time."

"What kind of security do you think they'll have?"

John chuckled, "Plenty." He began rummaging in his pocket and withdrew an envelope. "That's why I have these." He tossed the envelope into Gavin's lap. Gavin pried open the flap of the unsealed envelope.

"What the hell are these?"

"Temporary tattoos."

"I kinda' figured that out. But what are they for?"

"These are our tickets in. All of the Peelers have one. We couldn't pull off pretending to be a Gläm. They know when they're around each other."

"So, how do we….?"

"Put 'em on. I got a bottle of water in the glove box. There's a bunch of McDonald's napkins in there too. Get one wet for me too. Hold 'em on the back of your neck and presto, free admission."

Gavin grabbed the water and jostled things around in the glove box, moving the journal and the vehicle's manual to retrieve the napkins.

"Where did you find these things?"

"Find them? I made them with my printer." John sported an air of satisfaction.

Gavin poured water onto the napkins. He set up one for John, too. He placed a wet napkin in his uncle's hand and layered a temporary tattoo on top of it. They both, in an unplanned simultaneous act, held them to the back of their necks.

"Crack your window. They gotta be dry by the time we get there or we'll be done before we get in the door."

"How do we show these to them?"

"Just watch everybody else. You'll see. Peelers line up and just sort of bow their heads." John tilted his head sideways and down while driving to demonstrate.

"So, say we get in, then what? How do we find Nathan?"

"For lack of a better phrase, it's a snatch and grab. He'll be with Xavier, he's like the talent scout or recruiter for New York. Only problem is he's never alone. He'll be surrounded by people. He always is."

"What happens if they recognize us?"

"You run like hell. I'll hold them off."

"Are you kidding me? That's your plan." Gavin unconsciously slapped his leg in disapproval. "What movie were you watching when you came up with that? Do you expect me to just leave you?"

"Yes. You damn well better leave. Run as far and fast as you can." The fire was in his voice and a gravelly quality in his tone had surfaced.

"Why? We would stand a better chance making it out together." Gavin's voice became childlike, almost pleading. John heard and understood.

"Gav, they don't want me. I'm a thorn in their side but of no use to them. They need you or your brother and I won't let them have either of you. So, when the shit hits the fan do like I said. Run."

He turned onto West 13th Street. John's pickup slowly prowled the tight side streets, his side mirrors narrowly missing parked vehicles. He saw a line of people heading into a brownstone with some guys out in front of the loading dock examining them.

"That's it."

He swung into a spot on the side of the street. He reached across Gavin's knees and into the glove box, lifting out a pile of maps and napkins and pulled a nine-millimeter Beretta out. Gavin was speechless for a moment. Uncle John tucked the gun between his belt

121

and the small of his back as he got out of the truck. He let his flannel shirt hang out over it.

"What are you planning on doing with that?" Gavin asked as he exited.

"How did you think I was going to buy you some time, ask them real nice?"

"Aren't you afraid it'll go off?" Gavin asked as they diagonally crossed the street between traffic.

"The safety is on. Just worry about getting in the door. Pull your sleeves down." Uncle John performed the action as he gave the instruction.

"Why?"

"So they think you've been peeled. No more questions. Just keep quiet and follow my lead."

Their conversation broke off as they joined in at the back of the line. None of the other people in line spoke. The Peelers all had a dull glaze in their eyes and their bodies seemed older than their years. Many of them seemed to shamble forward in line using the brick wall as a guide. They were split about three-quarters female to one-quarter male. The line was moving along pretty quickly and soon Uncle John and Gavin were about six to eight people away from the doormen on the loading dock.

* * *

Inside, the conversation with Nathan had been moved to

more private quarters, an anteroom off of Xavier's lounge. The room was lit with an eerie greenish glow as if light was being filtered through pond scum. As they entered, two men appeared from either side of the door they had passed through. They had been waiting inside the room and keeping watch. Xavier ushered Nathan to what appeared to be a dentist's or a barber's chair in the middle of the room. Beside it a cylindrical object half as tall as a man was shrouded in a sheet of black silk. Nathan noticed that the chair appeared to have restraints as well as some sort of anesthesia apparatus. Xavier motioned for him to sit.

"I don't know…" Nathan stammered and backed away from the chair. The two men from the doorway moved to block his exit.

"Oh, I disagree," Xavier cooed. "I think you know very well that deep down this is what you want and it is what your father would have wanted."

Nathan acquiesced, moving to and sitting in the chair in the manner of a scolded child. The two men moved quickly and efficiently, apparently unencumbered by their expensive black suits. One of them secured Nathan's feet while the other secured his hands. Xavier smiled in appreciation. He turned to the cylinder and withdrew the black sheet. The first thing that struck Nathan was the radiance of the bubbles rising within the greenish glow. Then movement within caught his eyes, a twisting rubbery black thing like a snake or eel undulated inside. It turned to face him.

"No! No way are you putting that thing in me!"

He was in horror; he struggled against his restraints but to no avail. Xavier reached for the mask to deliver the anesthesia.

"I most certainly am going to." A smile still spread on his face as he pushed the mask onto Nathan's face. "In the end, you'll thank me."

Nathan began to lose consciousness. His vision dimmed and the last thing he saw was Xavier turning to a small steel table being wheeled across the room by one of his assistants. He turned back to Nathan with a gleaming speculum, intended to keep his mouth open for his guest. Nathan sunk into blackness before he could experience his mouth being forced open. Xavier put the device in place and nodded to his assistants. They moved to the cylinder and began removing the lid. Xavier left the room shutting and locking the door behind him. He returned to his seat and motioned for Allura to join him. She walked quickly to his side and knelt next to him.

"You have done very well. Nathan will be perfect." He patted her head in approval.

"I am pleased all has gone to your liking." She hesitated, then, "But Larson has been killed and Gavin and his uncle are outside as we speak."

"I was aware of Larson being killed; I knew it the moment it happened. It is a shame to lose a Brother, but he was only in the first cycle. I was not aware of the presence of Gavin and the uncle." Xavier paused for a moment. "Tell your men to allow them to enter. The brother is of no use to us, he is weak. The uncle is a threat and will be dealt with accordingly. They will be allowed to enter and move freely about the place. Nathan will be complete in a matter of minutes and should not be disturbed. When our two interlopers make it here, we'll deal with them."

"I understand." Allura stood and began to take her leave.

"Allura," Xavier called her back to him. "Gather my Brothers from the adjoining rooms and have them come here."

Allura bowed her head in servitude.

"And Allura," Xavier smiled wickedly. "Ask them if they are hungry. We shouldn't let Gavin and his uncle go to waste."

DISAPPEARANCE

Madson had begun to notice that Becker was becoming more and more distracted after leaving the Cross house. He knew his partner was a thinker. Becker would often become silent while figuring out how details fit together but this Cross case had his head spinning. They had found an address book in the study and Beck's nose had been buried in it all the way to the golf course. This case had both of their heads spinning.

Some commotion drew Madson's attention as some of the State Troopers at the scene were shouting directions. The FBI was now on the scene and would soon begin ushering any local law enforcement away from the investigation. Madson figured he and Becker should get out before they were thrown out.

"Hey Beck, let's get outta here."

Becker was still lost in thought but managed a grunt of a response in the affirmative. They moved through the crowded crime scene and abruptly stopped and regarded in silent awe the pile of body bags accumulating.

"Guess this makes up for the one we lost, Madson," one of the crime scene guys hollered.

"You bet!" Madson had no idea what the guy was talking about.

"What are you talking about?" Becker was direct and agitated.

"Whoa, Beck," as he was backpedaling in his white jumpsuit, "I didn't lose it."

"Lose what?" Madson growled.

"The Crossbody."

"Where is the Crossbody?" Becker grabbed ahold of the guy's shoulder.

"Easy guys, I got no idea where it is. A call came in about half an hour ago. Just before the Feds showed up that the body went missing."

Becker let the guy loose and began walking briskly to the car. Madson quickly stepped to catch up with him.

"I think I'm starting to get it, Beck."

"It's a mess, a real big mess," Becker added.

"Do we take this one all the way?"

Becker thought for a moment. "We could leave it to them." Becker glanced back over his shoulder at the bustling scene. "But I don't think I can walk away from this one."

"Me either."

"That settles it then." Becker nodded, unable to hide his appreciation.

"Certainly does." Madson was smiling as he grabbed the car door handle.

DEBACLE

John and Gavin tried to appear inconspicuous and small. They were next in line and trying to keep their cool. The thick-necked doorman motioned to John who bowed in turn and presented his marking. The doorman peered over the top of his sunglasses and nodded in approval. Gavin presented his tattoo directly which led to a painful pause in the inspection process. Gavin's mind raced as the thug intently held his hand to his earpiece. He nodded and waved the two of them into the club and motioned to the other bouncer to allow them in.

They walked through the darkened corridor between throngs of strung-out Peelers. They bellied up to the bar and sat down. The bartender brought them two bottles of water and indicated they should take a number like at the deli. The apparent process was that they would be notified when it was their turn to be fed upon. Gavin leaned into John to ask what the next step was as he noticed the bouncer walking quickly up behind them. Gavin saw the blue flash of the Taser as it was pushed into the back of John's neck. His uncle instantly slumped to the floor, and in a panic, Gavin grabbed at the taser and thrust it backward into the goon's guts. A simultaneous clicking shriek rose up from all the Gläms in the club. Apparently, due to their unique type of parasitic relationship, electricity was particularly painful to them. Gavin was stunned but remembered his uncle's words:

"So, when the shit hits the fan, do like I said. Run."

Amidst the momentary distraction, Gavin pushed his way through the reeling crowd of Gläms and past the dazed Peelers. He burst out the door and leaped off the loading dock. He sprinted to the truck, grabbed the spare key from the wheel well, and within seconds was peeling out into the street.

Gavin was sweating. His mind was spinning out of control. His hands were shaking on the wheel. He had to get away. He couldn't go back north, they would be looking for him there. He wanted to see his wife and daughter more than anything right now. He was aware that he might be dead if they caught up with him. He needed to find his way back to I-87. He decided he would head north and see them even if from afar for a moment. He would need some supplies from the cabin but was afraid they would be watching it. Deep down he was devastated at the loss of his uncle but with the adrenaline pumping the grief would hit him later. For now, he needed to drive and hope he wasn't being tailed. He would take the Northway up to White Plains and cross over to the Taconic. Less traffic and it would be easier to spot a tail with all the winding roads. There's an old truck stop over near western Massachusetts, Diesel Dan's, he would spend the night there before heading back to see his estranged wife and daughter. He would wake in the morning, unlike John. It would never make the newspapers but John's body would be found floating face down in the Hudson. His face was badly beaten and bruised his body naked and skinned from the neck down.

AWAKENING

Nathan woke in darkness. He rustled on what appeared to be an overstuffed sofa. His head felt heavy and his neck stiff. A dim gleam of light was peeking out from the edges of large windowpanes covered with Roman blinds. He struggled into a sitting position, prying himself from the folds of the upholstery. His feet were dangling over the side, toes barely touching the floor. His head felt like it weighed a hundred pounds, so he let it hang while rubbing the back of his neck. A low mumbling groan escaped from him as he stretched his neck to the left and right.

"You're awake," Allura spoke softly from the corner of the darkened room.

"Before you try to speak, drink some water. You will be hoarse for a day or two."

Nathan looked about the room and could see nothing in the gloom. Allura was steadily edging open the blinds and by degrees, the room was lit by the light of the city. Beside the sofa was a large bottle of mineral water which Nathan seized and unscrewed the cap. As he began drinking his throat felt instantly better. It was heavenly as if his throat was being blanketed in silk. An odd sensation of pulsating colors was playing out behind his eyelids as he slugged down the water. The whole experience of something as simple as drinking water was nearly ecstatic. Once again a small groan escaped from his lips as he used his shirt sleeve to wipe his mouth.

"It would seem that you both were thirsty. You'll need to keep hydrated; your guest will require a fair amount of additional water."

"Where are we?" Nathan croaked as he craned his neck and squinted at the city scene outside the window. "This looks familiar."

"It should," Allura replied with a half giggle. "We are in your office building. We're just one floor above where you work."

"How…" Nathan's voice creaked to a stop.

"Save your voice. Sit back and listen for a while. First of all, our driver brought us back here and he and the young women you met earlier this evening helped bring you up. Don't worry, no one saw. We have been in residence in this building for quite a long time and we have access to a private elevator. Xavier has this entire floor to himself."

Allura paused and in the pale glow of the city light, she looked down at her feet for a moment and nodded her head as if confirming something. She snapped out of the digression as if scolded to get back on track and began again.

"You will need to make certain modifications to your diet. Any drinks or foods that are high in salt or would dehydrate your Gläm are highly discouraged. Filtered or bottled waters are best. I would caution you that if you upset or neglect your ward it will be quite unpleasant for you. You are linked together and you will realize as you both recover that there must be a symbiotic understanding. You will be more aware of him as he becomes adjusted to you. You will also crave copious amounts of protein, sushi, and rare meats. What is most important is that your Gläm is provided at least once a week with human material."

"What?" Nathan was appalled and confused.

"You must find a Peeler; someone healthy and drug-free to feed on. Your Gläm will know what to do when the time comes. He will be very hungry once he wakes. He has been in stasis since your father's death. He and many others have been right in the next room above your head each workday. His brothers are waiting, some in the second or third stage, many more awaiting a first placement."

"I have to eat someone?"

"No. Well, not all at once. Just a little each week. They will feel no pain. Actually, the Gläm secrete a euphoric and addictive fluid that will make your Peeler eager to return to you. The initial feeding may be troublesome, but be sure to feed in an area that can be easily concealed. The upper thigh, torso, or back work well."

Allura looked down again as if receiving some unheard message.

"Well, you must be on your way now. Xavier needs my assistance back at the club. We'll be in touch regularly."

Allura raised both sets of blinds allowing the lights of the city to pour in and moved briskly to the door and swung it open. She motioned to Nathan to follow. He strained as he rose to his feet. As he dragged his tired frame to join her at the door he was awestruck. Beyond the comfort of his recovery room was an industrial space. A security guard and a lab technician were sitting in an elevated observation area paneled by glass. They worked in the subdued glow of dozens of monitors. All around them in neat rows were hundreds of Gläms in Plexiglas canisters like the one Nathan's Gläm was in. They lay still in their stasis, a pale green glow pulsing in unison from each one as they breathed, dreaming and waiting.

PREPARATIONS

Gavin woke at Diesel Dan's with a thundering headache. He had crashed into bed and all the adrenaline pumping through his system the night before had left him hurting and on empty. He had gathered everything he could from the cab of the truck and thrown all of it into a backpack. He dumped the contents onto the bed and began rummaging through it. Thankfully there was a bottle of Tylenol in the glove compartment. He swallowed a handful and guzzled down the remaining bottled water from the truck. He tried to concentrate on the items strewn across the bed but his vision kept going double. He stumbled into the bathroom and let the water run cold. He splashed his face repeatedly till the fog parted, then dried his face and hands and went back to assess what he had collected.

The journal was there still, which was good. Uncle John's wallet and keys were there along with an extra flannel shirt and a bandanna from behind the seat. His work gloves and some road maps, Gavin grabbed the gloves and shoved them into his back pocket.

There was a baseball cap from The Streaking Moose which he slid onto his head. He snatched up the maps, bandana, and flannel shirt and began to shove them into the backpack and as he did a small set of keys fell onto the carpet. The TUFF BOX logo was etched into them. Gavin quickly shoved the rest of the assortment into his backpack and still clutching the keys, dashed out of the room. He bounded down the stairs passed the garish red walls covered in imposing farm tools and sprinted to the truck. He hopped into the truck bed and fumbled with the keys in the lock of the cargo box behind the cab window. He opened the box and was filled with a rush of relief as Uncle John had apparently made preparations for their journey. The contents inside were proof enough of that.

Gavin unknowingly began to weep. The loss of his uncle had been so sudden he hadn't processed that the only person who didn't think he was crazy was gone.

Crouched there in the bed of the truck, he opened the cargo box. Inside he found a black duffel bag as well as a large rubberized toolbox. He was immediately feeling self-conscious so he tried his best to be nonchalant and scooted to the cab of the truck after closing the box. He tossed the bags onto the passenger side of the seat. He opted to drive a bit before investigating his discoveries. Distance and constant movement seemed like good concepts in keeping ahead of the Gläm. He drove a bit on I-90 West and jumped on 87 North and at a rest stop shortly after getting on I-87 he pulled off the highway to look through the bags. He pulled the truck into a spot near the off-ramp heading back onto the highway. It provided him with a fair amount of privacy. No cars on either side of him and most of the activity was centered around the rest stop bathrooms and vending machines a good ways away. He opened the duffel first and upon working the zipper he instantly found a note left by uncle John.

Gavin,

If you are reading this you are either snooping in my things or things have gone poorly in trying to reach Nathan. Assuming you are not looking through my stuff we have been separated or I am dead. If the latter is the case, please do not grieve for me as I knew going into this that I wasn't bound for a Disney vacation. I would ask that you do the memory of your Mother justice by assuming the role of Servator and continue in trying to undo as many of the Gläms' plans as possible. I know things have been hard for you but there are things going on here that are way bigger than any of us.

Inside the bag you will find nearly a grand in cash that I have collected from hosts I dispatched. From here on out credit cards are bad ideas as they can be traced, you will also find the pink slip for the truck try to ditch it for something else. There is also a new journal for you to begin some clothes, jerky and water. In the tool box you will find a gun and some ammo, a good fixed blade hunting knife and sheath, binoculars and a general set of tools. I have also given you a sharpening stone and a gun cleaning kit. You will need to become proficient in maintaining what you have. A solid flashlight, glow sticks, matches and a few lighters tucked into Ziploc bags to keep them dry are on the bottom. I tried to throw in what I thought you could use.

Despite how bleak things may appear there is a silver

lining. First you must understand that Nathan is now beyond our reach. Once he has become a host there is no going back. But although he is lost to us something can be gained from all this. He is a third stage Gläm and as is custom as many advanced stage and Immortal Gläms that are in the area will hold a gathering to celebrate one of their Brothers moving to the third stage. This presents an opportunity that comes along only once every twenty or so years. I had hoped to be there to help you; you won't be able to pull this off alone. You will need to find someone you can trust to help. With all of them gathered together in one place we can strike a blow that would set them back in their plans for the East Coast for years.

I am sorry I couldn't be there for you. Be strong.

~John

Gavin sat there for a moment. It was a lot to take in. His life would never be the same again. Part of him, a little nagging voice, still questioned his sanity. It made him wonder if all of this was just the final leap over the edge into madness. He knew it wasn't, he had seen these things in person twice, once as a kid and John had been there with Dr. Larson. Two people couldn't share the same hallucination. This notion steeled his resolve and he put the truck in reverse and maneuvered back onto the highway. As he drove, he kept wondering who he could pull in to help. Most people would think he was nuts. He decided to risk running to his place for some things; a quick dash and grab. If that went well, he would head to the cabin and do the same. With Uncle John gone, they would probably assume Gavin would run scared, at least he hoped that was what they thought.

138

WARNING

When Madson and Becker arrived at the Cross home, the police tape was twisting like a maligned serpent in the wind. It had been cut, not torn, which both detectives silently noticed. The door was open just a crack but that was enough to know that someone had been inside and very well could still be on the premises. The duo approached the door hesitantly. Their guns were not drawn but their hands were on the holsters. Madson stopped short of the door and looked back over his shoulder at Becker. Becker caught his glance and pointed at the door and made a twisting gesture with his free hand mouthing the word key. The door frame and jamb were intact; whoever entered the home of the deceased did not force their way in. Madson used his foot to slowly swing the door inward. He scanned the living room with his eyes. From behind the door a nine-millimeter pressed into Madson's ribs.

A hushed voice instructed. "Wave your partner in, move to the middle of the room and you'll both walk out of here alive."

Thrall

Becker noticed Madson go still and knew something was up, but he wasn't sure of what. Madson waved him in and moved to the center of the room. Becker drew his weapon and followed. He was met with a gun barrel at his temple as he crossed the threshold of the door.

"Holster your weapon and snap the clasp. Both of you."

The man behind the door waited to hear the distinctive sound and began to speak.

"I am going to back out the door and leave you both unharmed as long as you follow directions."

Madson and Becker were facing the fireplace and nodded slowly.

"There is no reason for you to be here. The Cross case is no longer your concern. You are not to pursue it any further. Do you understand?"

They nodded.

"You and your loved ones will be killed if you take any further action. We know everything about you and your families already."

Madson and Becker stood in silence for a full minute before they realized he was gone. The adrenaline and disbelief had left them lingering in thought after his departure. Madson turned his head towards the corner behind the door. Their mystery friend had vanished.

"That guy was educated," Becker mumbled rubbing his head.

"You mean he went to college, or he knew what he was doing?"

"Both."

"He said he knew all about us."

"I'd bet he does."

"You believe him?"

"I do because of his use of pronouns."

Madson was quiet for a moment. "Pronouns?"

"He most definitely used the word 'we.' 'We know everything about you and your families already' Was what he said."

"We... What does he mean 'we?'"

Madson and Becker stumbled out of the house and back to the car. They got in and shut the doors without speaking. They sat there in silence. A routine they so often repeated while working together, only at this moment they were dealing with an entirely new enigma, unlike anything they had ever dealt with before. Becker fumbled in his coat pocket for the address book. He flung onto the dashboard. They both stared at it as if some solution would pop out, some inkling as to what all this meant. Nothing came forth and it was Becker who finally spoke.

"What should we do with this?" He waved his hand in dismay at the book. "Give it to the feds?"

"I don't know, Beck." His voice was quavering, he swallowed hard. "He said he'd go after our families."

"He said we…"

"Yeah, he did, didn't he?"

"Sure did, 'we' as in more than one." A strange snickering smile began to spread on Becker's face.

Madson turned to look at his partner, wondering what was going through his head. "What is it?"

Becker sat up in his seat and slapped the book on the dash. "Our mystery man just gave us our only solid lead!"

"How do you figure?" Madson was genuinely lost and perplexed.

Becker was invigorated. "Hear me out, but first let's put some distance between us and this accursed house. I'm hungry. You hungry? Let's go to Compton's. Steak and eggs, my treat. I'll explain once we're there."

Madson was unnerved by his partner's giddy reaction to the scenario that had just unfolded but he trusted him. He always trusted him. And he was hungry.

Thankfully Compton's was nearly empty. Becker led the way to a booth in the back corner. Compton's was known for quick service and good food. A middle-aged waitress who smelled of cigarettes and perfume meant to conceal them headed over with a pot of coffee to fill their cups.

"Need a minute?" she asked while pouring.

"Two steak and eggs and the check." Becker's tone was terse.

"Got it," She responded unfazed; it wasn't uncommon for cops to be in a hurry.

As she moved towards the kitchen to place the order Becker leaned in to explain.

"Listen, I don't need to tell you that something big is going on."

142

Madson nodded in affirmative.

"But this is unheard of big. I know you are worried for your family, and so am I."

Again Madson nodded an affirmative.

"As scared as I am, I can't shake the feeling that I can't walk away from this one. Whoever is behind all this needs to be dealt with. We put bad guys away and these are the worst we have ever come across. Am I right?" Becker waited for another nod but Madson sat there looking at the wood-paneled wall blankly.

"The son, Gavin..." He spoke softly and quietly his mind somewhere far away.

"What about him?"

"We need to talk to him," Madson replied in the same distant tone.

HOMECOMING

Allura escorted Nathan down to a waiting car. The driver sat waiting for them with the car running. Allura opened the door for Nathan and briefly rested a hand on his shoulder. She handed him her card with her cell number on it.

"If you ever need anything, call me at any hour." She spoke intently and slowly to emphasize the statement.

Nathan was still a bit disoriented. He felt himself nod an affirmative. He lowered himself into the waiting sedan. Allura bent at the knees to stoop down to speak to him, her hand pressed against the tinted window glass. Once again her hand rested on his shoulder; she wanted him to look at her. He was nearly catatonic. She cared for him and was concerned but also needed to be sure he would be a good host. If anything went wrong with the Gläm's investment in Nathan, she would be held personally responsible. Xavier's contempt was a horrible thing and his rage was impossible to survive. Allura put some pressure into her grasp on Nathan's shoulder. He had been lost in the stark words on her business card:

> Ms. Allura
>
> Personal Assistant
>
> Concierge
>
> 555-2012

"Nathan," she shook his shoulder gently. "Can you hear?"

He nodded, still transfixed on the card. He was overcome by the feeling that he had just been swindled. He had traded his life for a monstrous partnership and was patted on the back and sent on his way. He now had his own little Lilith, a nanny for monsters in training. He was being sent out into the world to fend for himself and had the feeling that he would be watched carefully to ensure he followed the rules.

"Nathan, you must be sure to feed soon. Your charge will be hungry as the process of readapting to a new host is taxing on his system."

"Yes, he's hungry," Nathan heard himself croak.

"Be sure to take care of him and call if you run into any trouble."

"Okay."

Allura shut the door and gave the driver the address. The car pulled away and headed towards his apartment in Franklin Square. It was nearly morning and his fiancé would still be sleeping. Alice would have been tossing and turning waiting for him to come home. He would need to come up with an alibi for his whereabouts. She would buy whatever he told her. She loved him with a childlike adoration and naiveté. He began to rehearse a story but a low murmuring voice kept pleading with him. "Feed. Feeeed."

After the sedan had pulled up in front of his apartment building, he got out and moved to his door. The driver waited to be sure he got in safely and pulled away. He went upstairs and tried to quietly turn the key in the lock. He removed his shoes once he was inside and immediately began rummaging through the fridge.

In the bedroom, Alice was waking up. The rattle of the condiments in the swinging refrigerator door pulled her from her slumber. She woke and stretched then realized Nathan had not come to bed. She was in a tangle of sheets and a light blanket. She pried herself free and headed to the bathroom to relieve herself and to check on Nathan. Upon hearing the flush of the toilet Nathan was aware that she was awake, and his senses were on full alert. He felt like an animal in a cage trapped, caught and escape was impossible. He was unsure of where such a strong reaction would spring from. He was afraid of Alice's disfavor in light of his not coming home all night but this was something different, something stronger.

Nathan was unaware of the grating clicking sound emanating from his open mouth. His head still stuck in the fridge.

"You made it home! You had me worried hun'."

Alice rubbed his back as she spoke.

"What's that noise? Is the fridge broken?

He slammed the door closed and grabbed her by the

shoulders. In an instant, his hands were crushing her shoulders and the Gläm was at her throat, its addictive poison in her jugular. She swooned as it fed on her pale throat. He held her in a tragic embrace while his charge sated himself. His life wasn't the only one unalterably changed by the decisions made in the late hours of the night. This one last twisted gesture of affection would be the last embrace the two of them ever shared. Alice slowly slid to the floor unconscious. Nathan moved with her to the floor, his Gläm working at her throat, his body in such a state of euphoria that he would pass out on top of her as his ward finished its glut. If someone were to walk in and see them there, a mound of two young people in the kitchen, they might mistake it for a touching scene after a late night of carousing. But no one would walk in. No one would save Alice from the thing at her throat. This scene shared by the two of them, like many more to come, was anything but touching.

CHANCE ENCOUNTER

Madson hadn't been having any luck reaching Gavin by phone, so he decided to try catching him at home. The two detectives had spoken little to one another since leaving the diner. The drive out Route 29 East had taken about twenty minutes and the duration of the drive had been nearly silent. Madson finally broke the silence as they passed through Schuylerville and continued on 29 towards Greenwich.

"Years ago…" He paused his head swimming in the past. "Years ago, I had a run-in with Gavin and his Dad."

"Really, what kind of run-in?" Becker seemed eager to discuss the possibilities.

"It really didn't hit me until now. I can't believe I didn't think of it sooner. But when Gavin was just a kid, I responded to a 911 call at their old house in Wilton."

"What was it all about?"

"He had walked in on his Dad and a woman. He had just lost his Mom and was pretty shaken up about it. I don't remember much else. I took the boy to his Grandma's place for the night and put in a phone call for him to see a counselor. He went to see that hippy-looking guy, Larson."

"That whacko, why him?"

"Don't recall, I think Larson took him on. One thing I do remember, it's funny what comes back to you, is that the boy was petrified of his father and refused to be alone with him. He was going on about how his dad was somehow hurting his lady friend. At the time I thought he was just upset or confused about two adults having relations. Now it makes me think as to what that poor kid really saw that night."

"You think Cross was up to no good?" Becker mused.

"Back then, not at all, but now after all this I think maybe he was." Madson put on his blinker and turned down the long dirt drive to the house.

"Truck's here." Both men regarded that the truck was turned around pointed down the drive and it was still running. Without any hesitation Madson pulled the car across the drive, blocking the way.

Inside, Gavin heard the vehicle and grasped the 9mm tucked into the back of his jeans. He moved to the window and pulled the curtains aside a crack to peer at his visitors. He wasn't certain but they didn't look anything like what he had run into with his uncle. Far too normal, he figured they were cops. More than likely they were here about back child support. He pushed the gun back down into his waistline and tried to flounce his flannel to cover it. He heard the sound of a car door shutting followed by another. He realized just then that he had left the door open. He heard the door swing open and dropped his chin to his chest in frustration. From the living room, he heard someone call his name.

"Gavin, are you home? It's Detective Madson and my partner Becker."

"Be right there." Gavin was puzzled as to why detectives would be there. He was also puzzled by why the man's voice sounded so familiar. He opted to tuck the gun into the bottom of his backpack underneath the clothes he had grabbed. He paused to make sure the safety was on. He threw the clothes on top and as he started to leave the room, abruptly stopped and almost unconsciously stuffed a small-framed picture of his wife, daughter, and himself from his nightstand as well. He closed the clasp on the bag as he walked down the hall and slung one strap over his shoulder.

Madson and Becker were waiting in the living room. Both men were middle-aged and appeared stern but kind-faced despite their occupation.

"Hey, how are ya?" Gavin extended a friendly handshake to them both, trying hard not to come across as tense.

"Good," Madson replied smiling. "I don't know if you remember me but we met some time ago, when you were a bit younger."

All at once in a rush of memories, Gavin knew his face, his voice, and when they had first met. He was thunderstruck, and even though things had been so very strange as of late, he never anticipated running into him, Madson his childhood savior. His bewilderment must have been evident to his guests as Becker inquired about his well-being.

"You okay? You look like you just saw a ghost." Becker cast a sideways glance at the door to be sure Gavin couldn't bolt past them.

Gavin tried to compose himself; he blinked several times before responding.

"Well, I just haven't seen this guy in years," Gavin chuckled gesturing to Madson.

"It has been a while. Sorry for your loss." Madson furrowed his brow at Gavin trying to read a response to the mention of his father's death. There was none. Not surprisingly; Madson figured that the two may have been estranged for some time. He moved on.

"Gavin, would you mind if we talked a bit about your Dad?" A real sincerity was present in Madson's voice that Gavin found he couldn't refuse.

"Sure. What about him?" Gavin moved to the sofa and carefully placed the backpack on the floor between his feet. He motioned for the men to sit and they did in chairs opposite from the sofa. A small drum table sat between the upholstered seats and Becker noticed a considerable coating of dust on it. He assumed it meant the place had been empty for a bit or that Gavin had been neglecting cleaning and was living here alone. Becker sat back in the chair crossing one leg over another as was his custom. Madson sat forward in the chair, his forearms on his knees. He leaned into the conversation about to begin.

Thrall

Unbeknownst to Gavin and the two detectives, a black sedan was parked at the end of the drive and behind its tinted windows two men were assessing the situation. The passenger was attempting to discern the goings on through a set of binoculars and was relaying what little he saw to the driver.

"It's those two cops from before," the passenger informed the driver, "I remember their car."

"Then we will come back later. Killing cops draws unnecessary attention, which we cannot afford right now."

"Agreed." The passenger placed the binoculars on his lap as the driver slid the car into drive and headed back toward Schuylerville.

As the conversation inside the house commenced, Gavin would not be aware that Madson had inadvertently saved him again.

MEMORIES

Becker sat with one leg crossed over the other, his right foot tapping out an unheard beat in the air. He desperately wanted to be questioning Gavin but knew it wasn't the right approach. Madson's fatherly tone as well as his previous experience with the young man's childhood trauma made it imperative that he be the one asking the questions.

"Gavin, I have to let you know that we are here sort of unofficially. Your dad's case has been taken out of our hands. But we felt as though there were some aspects worth looking into further and wanted to ask for your help."

"I'm happy to help if I can but, honestly, my Father and I haven't been close for years." Gavin looked down at his hands as they toyed with the excess black strapping of the backpack. In the instant that his gaze was downcast Madson glanced to Becker who encouraged him to proceed with his eyes.

"I know you and your Dad had a falling out. How long has it

been since you spoke?"

"We haven't lived together since I was a kid. I don't think we have really talked beyond an occasional phone call since then either." Gavin's gaze remained on the bag.

"I guess I hadn't realized that you guys had been out of touch since that night."

Madson paused in apprehension, worried about the direction the conversation was about to head. Again, he looked to Becker who encouraged him with an expression to push on. Madson was reluctant but knew time was an issue.

"What do you remember about that night?" Madson asked the question and felt the air in the room grow silent and heavy.

"It's been a while since then. Usually, people seem to be telling me to forget about what happened that night. You were there too. Why are you interested all of a sudden?" Gavin tried to hide his irritation but it was of no use. Some things were just hard to talk about, and that night in Gavin's mind was the beginning of a nosedive that lasted for years.

"Anything you might remember may be helpful." Becker could no longer hold his tongue.

"Anything would help," Madson added in an effort to soothe both of them.

"Well," Gavin started to speak still curling and uncurling the straps of the backpack with his fingers. "I was still a kid. Mom had already passed away. Nathan was off to school by then. It's a little foggy. I remember Madson over there." Gavin motioned to Madson with his head while still looking down at his hands. "He showed up to save the day."

"What happened before that?" Becker was now sitting forward in his seat like his partner with an intent look in his eyes.

"That part… well I heard a noise down the hall, talking but real hushed, people moving around. My dad was in his study with a woman. They were sharing an intimate moment." Gavin left out the part of the story that he thought would make him sound crazy.

"And that was it? That was all that you saw?" Madson asked nudging the dialogue gently.

"I'm not sure what I saw but that was about it."

The room sat in silence a moment before Madson spoke. He wrinkled his face and began to speak in a tone that had an edge to it.

"Gavin, I understand that seeing your dad with a woman would have been hard for you so close to your mom passing away. But I think that there was more to that night than you are sharing. Some parts you have pushed away in your head. Something happened scary enough for you to live with your Grandma instead of your dad. I won't call you crazy; lately, I think I am going a little nuts." Madson shot Gavin a half smile. "You can tell me."

Gavin sat still for a moment fighting the flood that was about to burst the barricades he put up in his head. It was of no use. He sprang to his feet and began to shout.

"He had a thing inside him. It was black and slimy and it was peeling the skin right off that girl. It was like he wasn't there, his eyes were rolled back and the thing saw me and started making a weird noise, so I bolted and dialed 9-1-1."

Both detectives sat slack-jawed and speechless from the outburst. Gavin was out of breath his chest heaving. He felt the room start to spin then tilt and so he plopped back into the sofa before he fell over.

After a few moments of contemplation Becker asked the first of many questions that would follow Gavin's eruption.

"So, he had some kind of creature inside him and it was taking the skin off the woman?" No sooner had the last word left his lips than he turned to look at his partner.

Madson returned the look with a shrug of acquiescence. He turned his head to speak to Gavin who was staring off into space still breathing in a ragged fashion.

"Hey, Gavin," Madson waited for him to look his way. "You know what? After the last couple of days that doesn't sound crazy at all. It actually makes more sense than you might think."

Gavin smiled despite his exasperation. "I couldn't agree more."

Becker felt like he was missing something, so he interjected. "Is there something I am missing? Is there more to the story that you haven't told us?"

Gavin's head was spinning with a sort of catatonic elation. "You wouldn't believe the half of it!"

"Try me." Madson chuckled in response.

"How much time you got? It might take a while." Gavin stood slipping the backpack onto one shoulder.

156

"As long as it takes," Madson replied.

Gavin nodded in agreement. He gestured for them to wait a second. He walked out to the truck and extracted the journal and the dead Gläm from amongst his things. He left the gun in the truck so as to not arouse suspicion. When he walked back to the house both men were standing by the door waiting for him to return. They were either anxious to hear what was next or making sure he didn't take off. Gavin hoped it was a little of both. He led them to the kitchen table and motioned for them to sit. Without saying a word, he dropped both items on the table and turned his back to them to start making a pot of coffee. The detectives were once again silent. Gavin extracted three mugs from the cupboard. He set one next to each person and he sat down.

The three men would talk till it grew very late. By the end of their discussion, Gavin had found the help he needed in pursuing the Gläm and the detectives discovered the answers they had been searching for. The next morning Madson and Becker would request vacations. Their families would indeed go away, but both men had arranged to stay behind. They had business to attend to.

DISMISSAL

Gavin was parked across the street. John's truck had delivered him from the city and back upstate safely and for that he was thankful. He knew he could not directly see Linda and Clara. He worried about whether or not he was being followed or even whether or not they would have been watching the "girls." Besides their safety, he was also late on his child support as well as the fact that his wife already thought he was nuts. So, his retelling of the events that have unfolded over the past few days would only reinforce her opinion of his mental state. He simply could not risk seeing them directly. So, he waited. He was worried someone would think he was a stalker or a pedophile as he sat there waiting. But foremost in his thoughts was whether or not they were alright.

His watch told him it was quarter after two. School let out at half past. His soon-to-be ex-wife would more than likely look at his showing up at school with disdain. He slid down in the seat and tried to make himself small. He was feeling pretty small. Things would only get worse from here. He would not be able to see Linda and Clara again. Uncle John is more than likely dead. Gavin knew that his life had been altered beyond recognition. He would have to find a way to hide from them. He needed to find a place to feel safe and there was so much more to this whole mess that he had questions about. He remembered the journal in the glove box. He had questions burning in his head but couldn't bring himself to pull out the journal. He knew the answers to his questions would be within but right now he just needed to see them. He remembered how Clara looked when she was born; a full head of hair, so perfect and tiny in his arms. He remembered his wedding day and how the sun made Linda glow as if she were an angel. Despite how hard he tried to keep it together his past kept creeping up on him. He never recovered from that night when he saw his own father with that thing inside of him. After losing his mother his father was nearly all he had left. Thank God for Grandma.

The rumble of buses pulled him from his reverie. The buses lined up in front of the school like a herd of yellow cattle. The sounds of children poured between the idling diesel engines. Linda's beat-up old blue Volvo pulled in behind the buses. She had needed to drive Clara to school when they moved out. She hopped out of the car and crossed at the back of it onto the sidewalk. She disappeared behind the buses before Gavin could get a good look at her.

He was sure she was still beautiful, a determined look omnipresent on her face. He still loved her so much it hurt. Her mother-bear instincts couldn't be averted any longer. Gavin was a liability to her and Clara, now more than before. Linda did what she thought was best for Clara, for her safety, and Gavin couldn't help but love her for it despite the pain.

The buses began to pull away. They emerged hand in hand down the steps and towards the "blue bomber." Their arms swung in unison as Clara was motor-mouthing about her day. Linda was smiling a big broad the world is okay smile.

Gavin wept.

He covered his face with his hands and sobbed. Within his heaving chest, deep down in his aching heart, he knew it was for the best. All he could do was put them in harm's way.

As they piled in the car and pulled away, he straightened himself in his seat and watched them leave. A black sedan with tinted windows slid in behind them. As the windows receded two men in aviator shades sat in the front seats. The driver began scribbling on a pad and Gavin knew his fears were legitimate. He tried to convince himself they were cops but he knew better. The car was too nice, the men's appearance far too metro to be from these parts. Gavin quietly got out of the truck and trotted across the street. The men were busy watching Linda and Clara pull away.

Gavin ducked down behind the trunk and got onto his belly. He pulled his lock blade out and poised it against the base of the valve stem of the rear passenger tire. He waited on his belly for them to pull away and as they did, the damage was done. The valve stem was cut and they would be thumping on a flat very soon. He hopped up and brushed himself off hoping they were unaware of his vandalism as they were still watching his family drive ahead of them. The flat tire would buy them a smooth get away. The two of them would be hard for them to track down after the separation and the recent move. They were only leverage against Gavin if they were alive, that much was reassuring.

Gavin was resolved to disappear and as he nonchalantly walked back to the truck he was smiling. Moments ago, he was in tears and now he was puzzled by the feeling of elation spreading throughout him. Deep down he knew he wasn't losing them by leaving them. He was protecting them. He felt as though for the first time in his life he had clarity. Despite all of this madness, his head was clearer than it had been in years. He had a purpose. He would pick up where his uncle John had left off.

GONE FISHING

Gavin indeed had a purpose. He intended to coordinate with Madson and Becker. They needed a place to meet and make a plan, but Gavin didn't feel comfortable meeting up anywhere that could be connected to them or anyone else. He sent Becker a text.

-Meet?

A response came back within moments.

-Place?

Gavin texted back, he was intentionally brief.

-?

Becker texted back.

-SSPD 15 min

Gavin nodded in agreement. He wouldn't have thought of it. The Police Department seemed like a safe place to meet and make plans. Gavin drove downtown and parked in the lot diagonal from The Parting Glass. He waited in his truck hoping to use his mirrors to watch cars coming into the entrance. He spotted Madson and Becker as they pulled in. Becker was driving a blue Prius and Madson looked uncomfortable in the passenger seat at first glance. They pulled in next to him and Becker motioned for him to get into the back seat. Gavin opened the door and hesitated for a moment while he quickly scanned the interior of the cab. He turned and gestured to give him a second. He found more temporary tattoos in the glove box and slid them into the front pouch of the backpack. Beneath a pile of napkins, he discovered a cryptic note in black sharpie on one of them. He grabbed the note as well. After flipping down both visors and inspecting underneath and behind the seat he felt certain that he had everything. He closed the truck door and locked it. He climbed into the back seat of the idling car. The other half of the back seat was filled with fly fishing gear.

"All set?" Madson asked.

Gavin grunted an affirmative and Becker put the car in reverse and pulled out onto Lake Avenue. They drove past the firehouse and out Route 29.

"I just came from this way. Where are we headed?" Gavin asked somewhat agitated.

"Shushan," Becker replied, "wife's family has a cabin up there."

"What's with the fishing gear?"

"Good cover, tons of fishing on the Battenkill River," Madson added to the conversation.

"Cover?" Gavin mused.

Becker glanced at him in the rearview mirror. "Look in the creel."

The wicker basket contained no lures or bait. It was brimming over with shotgun shells.

ARRANGEMENTS

Allura let herself into Nathan's apartment. The door was open when she arrived. The place was silent save for the sound of her stiletto heels clicking upon the hardwood floors. The short hallway from the entrance opened into the kitchen space. At first, she hadn't seen Nathan and Alice on the floor in front of the fridge. The butcher's block had obstructed her view but the sound of Nathan snoring gave away their location. She stood there for a moment taking in the scene. She sighed as an unfamiliar emotion panged inside of her. She was genuinely perplexed as emotion was a luxury she had forgone long ago. For an instant, she felt remorse, or perhaps it was regret for the young couple sprawled out before her. Nevertheless, she cleared her throat loudly in an effort to wake Nathan. After the first two attempts were to no avail at rousing him, she reached down and gently rubbed his shoulder while speaking his name.

"Nathan," she cooed motherly. "We have much to do."

Gradually he stirred and was drawn back to this world by

her words. He had dreamt of swamps and seas and things deep below them. It was a strange type of sleep as he felt more like a voyeur of things seen in his own head. His head pounded as he rubbed the sleep from his eyes, it was as if he had the worst hangover of his life. His throat hurt incredibly and was terribly dry. Allura turned to the sink and reappeared with a pint glass of water from the tap. He greedily gulped it down before trying to speak.

"What do you mean?" He croaked. "What do we have to do?"

Allura shot Nathan a scolding look of disapproval. She held out a hand to help him to his feet.

"First let's get her to the sofa. She will be out for a bit."

Allura grabbed Alice's legs and Nathan hoisted her up beneath her armpits. The two shuffled her over to the sofa and endeavored to make her comfortable.

It was apparent on Nathan's face, as he stared at Alice, that he was concerned about her.

"One of my attendants will be here shortly, Paige, whom you've met."

He struggled mentally to place a face with the name. The events of the night seemed like a lifetime ago. As if on cue Paige appeared in the hall and moved towards them.

"Paige will remain here with Alice when we leave for the ceremony. She will stay here until it is clear that Alice has been acclimated."

Paige bowed her head as Allura finished speaking.

"Nathan, please pack a bag for the night. You will need a shower and a shave. Please dress appropriately as you will be meeting some very important figures this evening."

Nathan was moving into the bathroom and only when he spotted himself in the mirror did he pause. He took a moment to regard his reflection. The visage looking back at him was no longer his own. This realization overpowered his confusion and he resumed doing as he was told.

CARPOOL

Xavier was staring out the window of the Escalade when his phone rang. His thoughts were scattered despite his calm demeanor. He answered and put the call on speaker. "Allura?" he asked lackadaisically.

"Sir, I am at Nathan's now. He is preparing himself and we will meet you shortly."

"When?"

"Within half an hour, if that is agreeable."

"That will do." With that, he hung up the phone.

Normally, Xavier and his kind prided themselves on being far more patient than their human chattel. The current situation had him eager and somewhat anxious. Although he was an Immortal who oversaw one of the most prominent cities for the Gläm, he still reported to a superior. Xavier himself was not to be trifled with, those that existed beneath his power were very careful not to incite his wrath.

His superiors were as old as time itself and have been worshipped under many names; Cthulu, Tiamat, Jormungandr, Naga, or Hydra. Their presence has been known for millennia but as is the case so often the reality of myth is cast aside for the sake of comfort. The Gläm have always marveled at the ease at which humanity will disavow what is obvious simply because they don't want to acknowledge it. Xavier and his fellow Immortals knew that if they dared question The Old Ones' decrees they would be destroyed with a mere thought.

This was the case if his efforts with Nathan were for naught. He had assured his neighboring Immortals that Nathan's situation provided their kind with an opportunity for expansion. This expansion would provide them with a new seaport in the southern United States. Previously, establishing a birthing hive, like in New York City, Boston, D.C. and Miami was difficult in certain Southern communities, yet with the New Orleans hive thriving an additional location has become necessary. The purchase of an office building in Corpus Christi was set in motion a decade ago. The building's proximity to the water would allow for easy transport. There was also a parking garage and loading dock on the lower levels that would conceal the activity. Nathan would open a new office for Pendulum Accounting at this location. When, in time, he becomes an Immortal, he would oversee the area and ensure successful future acquisitions. Xavier's concern was that the timing was strenuous. Nathan had only been acquired very recently and so much was riding on his compliance. Xavier's peers and superiors felt that given Nathan's circumstances, a quick transition would deny him the opportunity to question his plight. His father's demise coupled with the rest of his troublesome family increased the urgency of putting some distance between him and them.

Thrall

"Sir," the driver's polite inquiry pulled Xavier back from his thoughts, "we have arrived. Would you care to wait or circle the block?"

"Waiting will be fine."

The driver put on the hazard lights as his counterpart in the passenger seat exited the vehicle and took up position at the front of the brownstone. Within moments Allura appeared with Nathan in tow. They were escorted to the rear door of the SUV and ushered inside. Allura sat behind Xavier and stowed Nathan's bag beside her. Only once Nathan was seated did their escort close the door and climb back into the passenger seat.

"So good to see you, Nathan," Xavier said grinning vacantly.

"You as well," Nathan spoke but it was as if the words were not his own. It seemed as though his thoughts were an afterthought. His mind flashed to his apartment when Allura instructed him to get ready. He was moving to comply before he had even thought of doing so. He was beginning to become agitated with this new fashion of existence. He felt as though his own will had been given a nosebleed seat in what was his own life.

"How are you managing your new arrangement?" Xavier posed the question in perfect timing. Nathan felt himself about to reply when Xavier raised his elongated and excessively knuckled index finger. He looked Nathan in the eyes and spoke telepathically to both of them.

"I'd like to hear how Nathan is doing. Forgive my Brother, Nathan; he is eager. You both must learn to work together. So much more can be accomplished that way."

With that Xavier lazily reclined again and asked out loud,

"How is it going?"

Nathan was dumbfounded. He struggled for words. He questioned whether or not what had just happened, had actually happened. Despite the frenetic pace at which thoughts were spinning through his head he managed to reply.

"It's a lot to take in," Nathan felt better once the silence had been breached. "I have concerns."

"Such as?"

"What will become of me… and Alice?" Nathan winced in emotional pain. Images of Alice raced through his mind, images of her on the floor unconscious after succumbing to him.

"Oh God," Nathan's hand clenched into a fist and covered his mouth. He was nauseous. Guilt slammed him silently.

"You and Alice will be fine," Xavier said in fatherly reassurance. "All will be taken care of. One thing is certain with our kind. We take care of our own."

AT THE CABIN

The drive was quiet for the most part, a brooding sort of silence persisted. The men were perseverating about the myriad possibilities of what would come. Gavin was still reckoning with his uncle's absence. All of the events of the last few days had left the three of them in a contemplative space.

As they made their way through farm country to the Battenkill River, Becker broke the silence. "We need to figure out where they are taking your brother."

Becker peered in the rearview mirror at Gavin as he spoke. Becker turned right before town and followed the river for a few minutes until the paved road subsided to dirt. The cabin sat beyond some corn fields along the riverbank. The place was nestled below some old oak trees; farmland to the left, the river ran behind it, and state forest on the other side. The area was secluded and privacy was almost certain as there were no dwellings nearby and only one way in or out. The driveway ran around the side of the cabin and ended below the shade of a large oak. Once they parked, all three men exited the vehicle and, without speaking, surveyed the property before heading inside. Again, when inside they checked each of the rooms and met up again at the kitchen table. The place was small; two bedrooms, a bathroom, and a combined kitchen and living room. A porch looked out over the river and a well-worn path led to its banks. Becker initiated the unloading of the car by grabbing two cumbersome hockey bags and laying them on the sofa. Madson and Gavin followed his lead and soon the kitchen table and floor space around the sofa were littered with gear.

"I am going to make a pot of coffee," Becker announced, "then we'll inventory the gear and figure out a game plan."

Madson grunted his approval and meandered towards the bathroom.

"How can I help?" Gavin asked Becker.

What happened next stunned and impressed Gavin simultaneously. Becker pulled a small notebook from his back pocket, flipped through a few pages, and reached in his pocket for a pen.

"As I call out an item, you locate it and give me an affirmative."

Gavin gave an apprehensive agreement as he readied himself.

"This may take a bit," Becker advised.

From the bathroom, Madson shouted, "So will this!"

The reply raised a snicker and shaking of heads from both men.

"At least shut the door!" Becker scolded.

"Too late for that," Madson responded.

With that Becker moved to the kitchen in order to open a small window above the sink. He returned to Gavin and began calling off items from his list.

"Two Mossberg shotguns…"

Gavin unzipped the first hockey bag and found a small arsenal within. He whistled a cat call nervously and wiped his brow.

"Check," he called out.

He could only assume that the other bags would be more of the same.

CONVOY

Xavier assured Nathan that all would be well as they fluidly made their way to Club Decadence. Upon arriving at the club Nathan was a bit surprised to see five additional black Escalades similar to the one he was in lined up outside the club. In each one, there was a driver waiting behind the wheel and an escort standing beside the vehicle. The other cars were all pointed towards the exit, Xavier's driver pulled up to the entrance and they were escorted inside. Nathan was puzzled and once again before he could pose a question it was answered by his liege.

"Introductions must be made Nathan, and we must snack before our trip."

In that moment as Xavier spoke to him Nathan saw a glimpse of something in Xavier as he finished speaking. His eyes appeared to have flashed as something moved quickly across them. The flesh about his head and neck seemed to shudder or quiver as if punctuating his comment. He turned back to lead them into the club. As they entered the club there were half a dozen men who were apparently security for those in attendance standing near the entrance and positioned inside as well. There were six men seated beyond the bar and they rose upon seeing Xavier. He outstretched his arms as he approached them.

"N' *kuubovN'zJ'yibP'uyz*," Xavier said.

Nathan heard the expression and although it was strange sounding, he somehow understood it. "Greetings Brothers," his internal companion translated as the information came in. His companion told him that this language is rarely spoken aloud, and only amongst brethren.

"Nathan," Xavier turned sideways, arms still outstretched, ushering Nathan towards the group of men. Nathan felt himself inexplicably bow his head to them.

"Brothers meet Nathan," his hand guiding him forward as he turned back closing the circle around him, "the next to join our ranks."

Nathan kept his head bowed despite wanting to look up. An audible clicking sound was rising in the room. His Gläm spoke to him. *They are applauding you, us. It is a sign of approval.* At that, Nathan was able to raise his head and greet the group of men around him. Xavier led the introductions.

The first was O'Balor, a broad, square-shaped, bald-headed man. Next a raven-haired Italian man with a Roman nose named Malvito. Then an immensely tall Russian who nearly crushed Nathan's hand in his own called Volk. A Japanese man with tattoos escaping his sleeves introduced himself as Oni. A wiry silver-haired fellow with a Spanish accent went by Brujo. Lastly, a Chinese man twirling his long mustache nodded to Nathan and introduced himself as Jiangshi. Nathan's hidden cohort spoke to him in a didactic way. *As you see we will retain a semblance of your previous appearance after our transformation.*

Nathan was intimidated; he knew he was being measured up by those surrounding him. He was also unsure if they were able to hear what his Gläm was saying to him as well. *They can,* came the reply. *And they will, always.*

PLOTTING

Once the cataloging of Becker's formidable arsenal and various supplies and gadgets was finished the men gathered at the table to formulate some kind of a plan. They essentially had little to go on other than Uncle John's book. Gavin had discovered a passage that had pointed to a Gläm resort of sorts located in the Catskills but John's research had not pinpointed a precise spot. So according to the Antiquus Libellus, the unfortunate next series of events would include Nathan being indoctrinated into the ranks via some kind of ceremony. The book also included that many other high-ranking members of the Gläm would be present including the Immortals of the area. According to what Gavin had read, things worked on a system similar to the feudal system of governance. An Immortal noble was in control of a large area with vassals or lesser ranked Gläm reporting to him. The assumption that Gavin was relying on was that Nathan would be with the representatives of the area when he was welcomed into the fold.

The men sat at the table, coffee in hand. The table was laden with an assortment of items: maps, binoculars, a laptop, cell phones, John's book, and two nine-millimeters.

"Catskills huh?" Madson quipped.

"That's what it says," Gavin replied, "just not where."

"Did your uncle say anything or leave any additional notes?" Becker asked, looking at Gavin's eyes hoping for something to dawn on him.

Gavin thought hard, he stood up and began pacing the length of the kitchen area. At that Madson also stood to go to the bathroom again. As he pushed himself from the table his coffee spilt across the maps. Becker cursed him grabbed some napkins and began dabbing it off the maps. Madson apologized as Gavin turned to see what had happened. As he saw Becker reach for additional napkins he exclaimed.

"That's it!"

"That's what? A bloody mess is what it is." Becker was obviously irritated.

"No, the napkins" Gavin raced over to his backpack and pulled the pile of napkins from the front pouch. He flipped through the pile till he found the one with two words scrawled on it in black.

"Glen Spey?" He spoke aloud puzzled.

"I think…" Becker began his right index finger scanning the coffee-soaked map laid out before him. "Yes! Here it is."

"Great," Madson added sarcastically, "but where specifically?"

"For that," Becker retorted astutely, "we need satellite maps."

SNACKS

After the gathered Immortals had given their approval and the introductions had concluded, Xavier turned to Allura and gestured to her to join the group. She moved with composed haste, her hands folded in front of her. She never raised her head as she approached. Xavier wrapped one arm around her and spoke in her ear; she nodded and moved towards the rooms at the rear of the club. Nathan watched silently as she softly spoke the name of each of their guests and motioned them to a room on either side of the hall. Lastly, she spoke to Xavier.

"Master..." Allura once again spoke without raising her head. "Your room waits for you and Nathan as you requested." She swept her hand from her midriff palm up towards the hall. Xavier wrapped an arm around Nathan and began walking towards Allura. Nathan's internal resident was quivering inside of him giddy with glee, excited to feed.

"I thought we could dine together," Xavier said.

Xavier led Nathan down the hall, behind the closed doors he could hear stifled gurgling sounds. His stomach was doing cartwheels; he wasn't sure if he would vomit or if it was hunger. As they entered the room at the end of the hall it was as he remembered. Three chairs, the largest in the center with women kneeling at the base of the one in the middle and on the right. Allura had been silently following. She moved to the seat on the left and sat demurely, hands clasped at the knee. Xavier strode to the center chair and plopped down; he motioned for Nathan to sit.

"I thought this may be an opportunity for you to practice as well as witness what it will be like for you later on."

Nathan said nothing. He moved to his seat; a young woman knelt at his feet her head hung down. It was as if there were matching statues on the floor in front of both men. He regarded her as she waited motionless barely breathing.

"Nathan your first feeding was hasty, you both were eager no doubt. Yet we must be wise. Feeding on such a visible spot as the neck must be saved for a final feeding as it is hard to conceal. Try for instance the upper arm or leg, even the hips or stomach. This is Beth, she is yours."

Beth rose to her feet. She never made eye contact. Before Nathan knew what he was doing he had raised her blouse. He was eye to eye with her navel as he felt the Gläm surge forward. The horrible clicking sound pounded in his ears as she groaned, ribbons of flesh unraveling from her stomach. Xavier watched, smiling in silence until Nathan was sated. When he pulled away from her, she collapsed in a heap on the floor.

"She will be marked as our chattel and will accompany you wherever you may go until you are through with her."

Xavier spoke very directly as he slid himself forward in his chair. He reached down and grasped the young woman by her chin. As she stood Nathan was able to discern that she had been fed upon heavily before, he wondered where Xavier could possibly find a place to feed.

It was then that he saw that shimmer in his eyes once more. He pulled the girl towards him her neck inches from his mouth. Nathan could not look away. In a flash, his eyes appeared to roll back in his head. White bulging sockets open wide. His lower jaw was distended or more-so elongated like a snake's. His tongue seemed to be possessed of an intellect of its own. It swelled as it stretched out; when the tip touched her flesh it shuddered and stood still. Sickle-shaped barbs sprang from each side of his tongue just before it plunged into her jugular. There was a brief gasp as she went stiff. Xavier's jaws clamped upon her throat. She appeared to spasm with each swollen swallow he sucked down. Nathan had no idea how long it took; he had been mesmerized. She too fell in a heap but was assuredly dead. He looked up from her corpse to see Xavier's face beaming in delight back at him. His visage was normal again. He wiped his face with a hanky daintily and rose to his feet.

"Shall we go?" He waved his hand to the exit, "I always find it better to have a snack before a long ride."

He enveloped Nathan again in a half embrace and rejoined his peers waiting in the hall.

RECONNAISSANCE

Becker leaped up and snatched a laptop bag from the sofa. He put the computer down on the table in the middle of the map and inserted a small USB antenna into its side before starting it up. It sprang to life, and he then got his cell phone to try and create a hot spot.

"Will you be able to get a signal?" Gavin asked.

Becker paused for a moment to look back at him.

"Hope so." After a moment he indeed did. It may have not been of the best strength but it was working, a tad slow but working.

Becker entered the name of the place into Google Maps and waited for the map to load. Madson pulled up a chair and spun it backwards, straddling it cowboy style, to get a better view. Gavin remained standing, leaning over the table, hands planted on its surface. The map of the area appeared on the screen at first blocky and glitchy but resolved itself.

"Okay," Becker began, "what do we look for?"

Silence prevailed for a moment. Then Gavin offered, "Water, they need water."

"Good. What else?"

"It would have to be a big place, right?" Madson puzzled, "with a fence."

Becker moved the scope of the map around the area; it was heavily treed and spotted with bodies of water. As Becker moved the map around from pond to pond and home to home Gavin suddenly blurted out, "Stop, there! Right there!"

His finger was pointing at a shape on the screen.

"Can you zoom in on that?"

Becker zoomed in on the spot. To the disbelief of the men there, created with carefully placed boulders, was the mark of the Gläm. The arrangement was adjacent to a palatial stone mansion and a large pond in the dead center of a large parcel of forest near to Bodine State Forest. Becker noted the GPS coordinates and entered them into his phone. It was already midday. Becker began packing away the laptop and maps. Madson remained seated as both men began packing up.

"So now what?"

"We leave," Becker replied while still working busily, "We want to get there before dark."

Gavin gave an affirmative, "Yup," whilst packing his things in his backpack.

"But we just got here," Madson whined.

"Let's go, we got to get there so we can figure out what to do next," Becker scolded.

Madson rose and shuffled to help with the gear on the sofa. He tossed the creel of shells into a hockey bag with a child-like frustration.

"I didn't even get to go fishing."

VOYEUR

Nathan was ill at ease after feeding. His benefactor and the other Immortals wasted no time in satiating themselves. Their eagerness allowed Nathan a small portion of privacy, his brief moment of hesitation went unnoticed. Once he was close enough it was out of his control, consuming was imperative to his Gläm, and it overrode all else. Everyone was whisked away and into waiting cars. The women they had fed upon left in heaps. Nathan was again seated next to Xavier and the line of vehicles swept into traffic with military precision and speed. The alacrity of the drivers was apparent and seemed to please Xavier as a slow subtle grin crept upon his face while he gazed out of the tinted window.

It also seemed that feeding sedated the Gläm. Nathan noticed that his internal companion was at ease and that Xavier had been contented. His connection was still fresh, so he did not share in the euphoria. When he contemplated what he had become it was unimaginable to him, yet he justified it with the promise of power and money. He wondered if what they had told him was really true. Would he enjoy the riches and power they had promised, would he remain as part of an Immortal once the time had come? Xavier must have sensed his anxiety.

"Just sit back and relax, we will be at the manor in Glen Spey in two-and-a-half hours. Get some rest, you will need it."

With that Xavier closed his eyes and reclined, settling quickly back to rest. Nathan opted to do the same. After feeding a sedated feeling took hold but his mind sank into frenetic glimpses of images drawn from his own memories and others. Flashes of what must have been his father's and his grandfather's lives spun around in his head.

Scenes of his own childhood from all three vantage points co-mingled in an eerie fashion. Then all became dark as he felt a crushing immensity of water all around him. He was aware that these were not his memories but his Gläm's.

An awareness of others nearby, of a group in fear as they were herded and collected away from some central point, overtook him. As they were whisked away blue glow swelled behind them illuminating the depths. In that moment of shared memory, Nathan was afforded a sight that seared his consciousness. The Source towered before him; it was stories tall, a multitude of tentacles gentling and writhing as if waving goodbye to its children. The overwhelming stature and sheer presence were too much for him and he was sent into an utterly unconscious state of sleep.

CONVICTION

As Becker drove Madson was snoring heavily. He rumbled and snorted like a disjointed locomotive, stuttering and stopping and starting up again. Becker drove fast but in a controlled fashion. Gavin was lost in his thoughts and was somewhat startled when Becker spoke.

"Are you sure about all this?"

"About all what?" Gavin was genuinely puzzled.

"About what we are about to do."

"I am not sure of what exactly we are about to do. I don't really know what will happen."

"Neither do I." Becker sighed. "I mean you could walk away from this. I can stop the car; you can get out and try to return to normal."

The statement hit Gavin like a freight train. He hadn't really spoken to Becker much through all of this. Honestly, he hadn't really heard him speak that much at all. Now out of left field, he hits him with this.

"I'm not saying you're not up to it," Becker paused searching for the right way to put it, "I just want you to know that you have options."

"What about you guys?" There was an edge to his response and Becker noticed.

"We're the good guys. The day we swore our oath to serve and protect our options were eliminated. For some, it's a job. For us, it was always more than that." For the first time since the conversation began, Becker looked into the rearview mirror at Gavin. "That's why we're partners."

"I appreciate the option, but I need to see this through to the end."

"Why?" Becker's tone was cold and flat.

"Why?" Gavin returned agitated.

"That's what I asked. Why do you need to see this through to the end?"

"Because they killed my mother, stole my dad, and now my brother. Because everything about them is wrong and somebody has to stop them." Gavin wasn't even all that aware that he had been yelling. He was vehement, his fists clenched and his chest heaving.

Madson woke up. "What the hell's going on?"

Becker once again made eye contact, "That's all I needed to hear."

Gavin chuckled at that and Becker, for the first time since they met, was grinning from ear to ear.

Madson returned to slumber just as quickly as he'd woken.

Thrall

Silence reigned again as Becker drove and Gavin stared out the window. They wove their way through quaint towns and hamlets and soon began weaving through winding roadways that climbed and dove between rock cuts and pocketed lakes till they had arrived at the Manor at Glen Spey. It was nestled on a large parcel of land near a state preserve. So, Becker drove by the long private road slowly and then down past it a few hundred yards to the entrance of the State land. There was an abandoned ranger shack at the opening of the rutted dirt road. They drove past it and campsites were speckled along the narrow lane. After half a dozen sites Becker stopped abruptly at a trailhead.

"There!" he exclaimed.

"What's there?" Gavin puzzled. "All I see is trees."

"Look up!"

As Gavin's and Madson's eyes followed the tree line upwards a fire tower reached into the sky.

"That," Becker began smugly, "is how we formulate a plan."

The men found the tower was stout and in good shape as they climbed to its peak. Becker had high-powered binoculars and was able from this vantage point to describe the manor to them.

"I'm actually looking right at the front door. It's a wide double-door entrance with two big bald guards posted. The driveway has got to be close to eight hundred yards long. There is a large parking area to the right of the house in front of the large stones arranged in a ring. There are a couple of cars in there already. Oh… a line of cars is pulling in now, we beat them here. Men are moving to the vehicles as

190

they park. They are escorting people to the main doors. Some of the others are being moved to a side entrance, looks like women mostly, and a large patio area with floor-to-ceiling glass windows. There's a shed or something butted up to it on the far corner."

Becker swung to the other corner of the platform to gain a better view. He peered through the binoculars at what lay inside and a plan came crashing down on him. He outstretched his binoculars to Gavin and Madson.

"That, gentlemen," he shook the binoculars at them, "is how we will end all this."

Gavin struggled to locate the area Becker was referencing, and then he saw it and it became clear what Becker intended to do. A five-hundred-gallon propane tank was nestled beside the manor.

Gavin chuckled and handed the binoculars to Madson. Becker was already climbing down shouting to the other two men. "Let's go, I figure it will take a half hour to hike to the tree line just below the house. I need five minutes to gather supplies from the car. By the time we get into position, they should be settled."

"Wait a minute," Madson grumbled, "I still don't know what the hell I'm looking at."

"Don't worry about it partner I'll explain on the way."

Madson groaned an expletive under his breath and began stomping down the fire tower after them.

CEREMONY

Xavier and Nathan were escorted to a large hall with a roaring fireplace set into massive field stones. The ceiling was vaulted, and a balcony wrapped around its perimeter. The hardwood floors echoed the footsteps of those in attendance. The space's southerly wall was almost entirely made of glass windows and opened up onto a spacious patio where women mingled with one another. After courtesies and greetings were offered the Immortals gathered in the hall. Guards came forth with robes, each of which was such a deep blue they at first appeared black. The robes bore the insignia of the Gläm in an embroidered gold thread on the chest. Nathan was given a red robe and Xavier was given a white one with golden panels that ran down from below the arms. The guards bowed as they offered the garments to them and then turned to walk away.

Once they donned the robes they arranged themselves in a circle in front of the fireplace. Xavier stood with his back to the blaze with Nathan at his right side. He outstretched his arms and addressed the group.

"*N' kuubovN'zJ'yibP'uyz.*" Greetings Brothers.

"*Ta Ny'ybobejuMiyYb'buv'lovn.*" My gratitude for attending.

The phrases translated themselves as they fell on Nathan's ears thanks to his ward.

"I present to you this evening Nathan Cross, Grandson of Augustus and Son of Charles, in time he will join our ranks as an Immortal brother and preside over our recently acquired area of Corpus Christi. Join me in celebrating his appointment as we present to him our highest symbol of distinction."

Allura stepped forward across the circle with a black lacquered box and slowly raised the lid before Xavier. A pale blue glow emanated from within, Xavier reached inside with both hands and brought out a golden chain and at its end a large pendant of the Gläm's sigil. It was made of gold as well but at its center, a vial of sorts shone blue. A small piece of what appeared to be gray flesh floated or writhed in the fluid.

"All hail the Source!" Xavier called, and the others echoed.

"All hail the Source, from whence we came!" He called and again they returned his proclamation.

"Let no one challenge the legitimacy of this appointment!"

With that Xavier placed the amulet around Nathan's neck, looking him deep in the eyes in such a way that it was clear that there was no going back from here.

CONFLAGRATION

Becker motioned with his hand for the men to crouch low as they neared the tree line just below the patio. The women on the porch were absorbed in each other's company and conversation. Becker whispered to the men in a hushed tone, and motioned for them to put their gear down.

"Here's how we are going to do this. I'm going to poke a hole in that propane tank. Then we wait for a couple of minutes and hope the ladies don't smell anything. Then we light it off and run like hell."

"How do we do that?" Madson quickly interjected.

Becker put his finger to his lips to keep him quiet. He carefully opened two ballistic cases on the ground. One held a high-powered rifle with a homemade silencer, the other a compound bow. Next, he reached into his backpack and pulled out a road flare and electrical tape.

"After the propane has had time to pour out, we shoot the flare onto the ground below it. I'll rig an arrow and we light it at the last possible moment before firing. Now which one of you is good with a bow?"

Madson shrugged and waved his hands in defeat. Gavin smirked, raising his hand reluctantly. Becker was wrapping the tape around the flare and arrow and once it was secure handed it to Gavin.

"Okay, Gavin you are going to have to make a kneeling shot from here. Madson, you'll light the flare and start heading back to the car immediately. I'll give you the go sign and do the same. Are we clear?"

The men nodded in approval. Becker took a peek through the binoculars to ensure everyone was still inside. He used a fork in a branch as a rest and aimed his shot. A rush of air and a ping of metal went unnoticed by the women outside. Becker quickly looked at his watch and began timing. After a minute he motioned for Gavin and Madson to get into position. Gavin drew back the bow and nodded again that he was ready, Madson held the igniter cap to the end of the flare. Becker signaled to them and the flare burst to life. It sailed halfway across the ninety-yard distance before those on the patio even noticed. When it struck, the three of them were already turned to run. The concussive force of the blast shook the ground.

The tank exploded through the wall into the hall and flames engulfed the entire patio, glass exploded outwards slicing through the women. Alice perished under a sea of glass. Inside flames roared, and smaller explosions rang out. Two-thirds of those in the hall were crushed as the propane tank flipped end over end after it rocketed through the wall. Beams fell from above as the buttresses and balcony collapsed smashing down on those gathered.

EVASION

Madson was gasping for air by the time they had gotten back to the car. They sped away in the opposite direction so as not to pass in front of the Manor. The smoke from the blaze rose above the tree line. Gavin was turned around looking out the back window watching the smoke rise. Sirens could be heard in the distance, but it would be some time before they arrived. The men drove until they reached Bethel. The ride was not victorious but solemn. Over a barbecue dinner, they agreed that they would go back home as if nothing had ever happened. Gavin would return to the cabin and only reach out if it was dire. They were unaware that their endeavors had not been successful.

* * *

At the Manor, chaos continued. Flashing lights and sirens dominated the scene. Nathan woke to Allura's face as she gently shook him. His ears were ringing and he was in severe pain on his left side. In the blast, he had been terribly burned. His left arm and the side of his face were blackened and screaming in pain, the sigil grasped firmly in his scorched hand. Xavier lay across his chest. He began to stir. From the look of things, he had a badly broken arm and leg. A beam fell in the explosion and Xavier must have leapt to shield Nathan.

"Indeed I did." Xavier groaned as he pushed himself up hearing Nathan's thoughts as they played out.

Despite his pain, he marveled as Xavier snapped his limbs back into place and dusted himself off around the room strewn with debris, piles of rubble lifted and parted as the Immortals in attendance gathered themselves up and reconfigured their bodies. The guards were beyond repair as were the vast majority of women on the patio. Allura had been spared the shower of glass shrapnel as she was watching the ceremony from the foyer. Now she regarded her master and Nathan with imploring eyes.

"We have to go!" she shouted.

Almost in unison those alive made their way to vehicles and went their separate ways. Police, fire crews, and paramedics made no effort to stop them. As they drove towards home Allura produced pain medication from the glove box and insisted Nathan take some. He struggled to oblige and within moments of taking it passed out. Once it was certain that he was settled Xavier finally spoke.

"It appears we have enemies…"

He paused, seething with rage.

"Enemies that we have underestimated, but who have also greatly underestimated us."

Thrall

He clenched his fist and held it to his mouth for a moment in an effort to control his fury.

"Allura get me all the records from Dr. Larson's office on Gavin Cross, we will deal with this personally to ensure Nathan's appointment."

The rest of the ride to Manhattan was silent. A team of doctors met them in the parking garage and took Nathan away to tend to his burns. He would heal with time but be scared. The flesh on his face and arm rippled from the flames and the insignia forever burned into his palm.

* * *

Gavin did not go directly to the cabin. When Madson and Becker dropped him off at his truck at the police station parking lot, he pretended to rummage around while they waved goodbye. He waited for them to leave and then got out of the truck, locked it up, and walked up the hill to Broadway. He went to the bank and had three cashier's checks made up. One was for ten thousand and the other two for five thousand dollars. A couple of storefronts down, there was an old-fashioned toy store. He wandered around inside for what seemed like an eternity to pick the absolute best teddy bear for his daughter Clara. He found an adorable one, a fawn brown with a pink, satin ribbon around its neck. He paid for it with the cash his uncle had left for him. Across the street, in the old Arcade building, there was a travel agent. Gavin arranged for a timeshare condo in the Poconos. He listed the participants as his wife Linda, the Becker family, and the Madson family.

Despite his concerns, he returned to his grandma's old house. He perused around for any effects or supplies that he might need. He grabbed a yellow legal pad and sat down at the kitchen table to write. He wrote notes to Madson and Becker to go along with the checks. He explained the timeshare and money were in case things got crazy, and they needed to place to get away to. He wrote a letter to his wife and daughter as well. He called his buddy Phlip from work and asked him if he wanted to be a delivery guy for a hundred bucks. He jumped at the opportunity. Gavin met with him and gave him directions and instructions to drop off the two envelopes and the bag with the teddy bear in it. Phlip was a little puzzled but nodded in agreement. He delivered the envelopes to Madson and Becker the following week outside the station. The bag with the teddy bear he delivered directly after meeting with Gavin. The note inside was for his girls.

Linda and Clara,

I miss you both terribly; unfortunately, it seems best that we don't see each other for a while. Apparently my dad was involved with some shady people in some questionable activities. He has left behind a mess I'll need to resolve. Please find a check inside to hold you over for a while. There is also information about a place in the Poconos should things ever get crazy.

Thrall

All my love, Gavin

P.s. The teddy bear is for Clara, please tell her I love her very much.

Check out this exclusive excerpt from the sequel to
"Thrall"

Enthralled

Out now on paperback and Kindle

Thrall

SLEEPLESS

Gavin couldn't remember the last time he slept through the night. He stared at the ceiling of the cabin's lone bedroom. Gavin questioned whether or not staying at his Uncle's place would be best. Months had passed since he had tried to destroy the Gläm forces amassing in the Berkshires. The deciding factor for him was that it was the best location to minimize collateral damage. If they came to hurt him here, they would find him alone. The same couldn't be said for his Grandmother's place.

The leaves had mostly fallen and it had started to get cold out. There was plenty of firewood to be had between his efforts and his Uncle John's. Yet no fire smoldered in the wood stove despite the chill. Even so, he was covered in sweat, his mind raced in circles around the unknown. There were still so many things left unanswered for him since becoming tangled up in the sinister affairs of the Gläm. His brother Nathan's whereabouts and condition were a mystery. Whether or not they had been successful in taking out the Gläm was also uncertain. He hadn't heard from Madson or Becker, which was probably a good thing. After all, sometimes no news is good news.

When they parted ways, they had agreed that contact was to be minimal. Becker had even insisted on a code word, *phantasmagoria*, to be safe. Or, perhaps just to show off his vocabulary.

Gavin desperately wanted to see Linda and Clara but he knew any contact with them would be dangerous. He hated the way things had gone with Linda. In his mind, he could hardly remember a time when he didn't love her. His daughter, Clara, was the best thing that ever happened to him. The day she was born was one of the most amazing things he had ever been a part of. Even though he knew that not seeing them was the best thing he could do to keep them out of harm's way, it still tore him up inside when he was alone with his thoughts.

A coyote yipped from the tree line. Gavin was up and on his feet in an instant. The sawed-off shotgun from his bedside table was in his hand before his feet hit the floor. His head cleared quickly and he realized what it was. He had tried to secure the cabin as best he could, setting up small alarms and tripwires so that any unannounced company would be revealed to him.

At times, he missed the convenience of more modern living but, given his situation, there were some benefits to being in the middle of the woods. At night it was dark, very dark, and if one didn't know their way around, there was a catastrophically strong chance that someone was going to trip or bump into something. The notion of having a natural defense of sorts, provided a small sense of security. Gavin found that at times he bordered on paranoia, but usually thought it best to err on the side of caution. He had seen first hand his enemy's capabilities. His Uncle John had perished right before Gavin's eyes as a result of underestimating the Gläm. When they took action it was sudden and devastating.

Gavin had found a box of Christmas ornaments in the back of John's closet. In it were strings of tiny bells no doubt meant for trimming a tree during the holidays. So, just like one of those corny kids' movies, he used fishing lines to construct tiny tripwires around doorways. In a matter of weeks, he had become accustomed to them, but there were a few mishaps after he had first installed them. Which, if anyone had been around, it would have been very funny to witness. He was content to chuckle to himself amid the commotion. His grandmother had always said that being able to laugh at yourself was important and in moments like those he couldn't help but think of her.

Gavin got himself situated back in bed hoping that sleep would soon come. He glanced over at the gun to ensure it was still there. It provided some comfort knowing it was at the ready. If it had been the tinkling of bells instead of yelps, he would have needed it. Laying there in bed, he would imagine how they would come for him; smashing through a window, kicking down the door and bursting into the room or overtaking him with sheer numbers and pinning him to his mattress. Gavin would envision their attacks and rehearse his retaliations in his head, most nights until the sun rose.

Tonight, his thoughts wandered into memory, remembering his Grandmother. They had gone to a zoo once when he was younger, where there was an exhibit that housed a Grizzly bear. It was a man-made reconstruction of a rock cave with a little waterfall and a honeysuckle bush nestled at its peak, all wrapped around by a cast iron fence. The bear was huge, even at a distance. Gavin remembered its eyes. They seemed lost and complacent. Every rock tossed, finger pointed, each poke and prod took its toll. The massive creature looked defeated and sat there staring back at him. Gavin remembered starting to cry and squeezing his grandmother's hand. She had been unaware that he was upset. She looked down at him and asked what was wrong, but he could not articulate a response. Nor could he look away from the bear. There was a longing that weighed on him but he still could not break its gaze. His grandmother had asked a second time but he did not hear her. Worried for him, she scooped Gavin up and headed toward the next exhibit. His eyes were still locked on the beast even as it became a shadow and eventually passed from his sight. Gavin heard it bellow as he left. He had never heard a bear roar before but somehow instinctively he knew that this wasn't one. He felt himself tossing and turning. In his dream, he was being pulled to look away from his grandmother. His gaze slowly drifted down to his hand, it was being held by someone. His vision followed up the wrist to the arm and there was Nathan. His older brother wasn't usually in this dream. Nathan wore a puzzled look as he stared back at Gavin. For some unknowable reason his gaze was unbearable.

No, Gavin knew fully well the reason he couldn't look his brother in the eye.

He writhed and twisted in his bed, drenched in sweat, restrained by the sheets and covers that were now curling about his limbs like tendrils.

"*You tried to kill me.*" Gavin heard, unmistakably, the voice of Nathan from their childhood.

Gavin shot up to a sitting position, sweaty and breathing hard.

He rubbed his hands across his stubbled cheeks, fixed his covers and pulled them up over his head like when he was a kid, trapped within an illusion of safety.

As he struggled to drift back to sleep a small grin stretched across his face because he knew now the plight of the bear.

Acknowledgements

First, let me express my sincerest gratitude to my family and friends for supporting and patiently tolerating me in my endeavors.

My Valenza Publishing family most definitely deserves praise and admiration for all of their hard work in helping my stories get out to the world, while also allowing me to be undeniably myself. Andrew has always believed in me more than I ever did myself. Dr. Hull, a kindred soul, keeps me on point. Mr. Gunther gets my aesthetic and makes my covers look badass. I appreciate the camaraderie, the sacrifices you all make, and the profound intelligence and creativity you dole out regularly.

I would also like to thank Chris and Jade for their reviews of Thrall. Your support and honest reviews helped the story gain traction.

I am ever so grateful to those of you who enjoy reading my stories. Rest assured that you are in for a wild ride.

About the Author

J.T. McGee is a former art teacher in Saratoga Springs, New York. He is an artist, adventurer, writer, and crafter. He takes great pride in the impact that he has had on his students over the years. Since J.T. was born in the wrong era and can't  charge headlong into battle, so instead he writes books and recreates ancient weaponry.

@mrbigbad76 on Instagram and Facebook.

Thank you for reading!

Please consider leaving a review for "Thrall" on Goodreads!

Follow us for more @valenzapublishing on Instagram, Threads, and Facebook!

And support indie authors by checking out these incredible books!

"Fate's Tether" by Jade Nioma

"A Voice of Life" by Lindsey Forkel

"Witness to the Revolution" by Kiersten Marcil

"The Maiden's Husband" by Morgan Christiansen